WULFIE

A GHOSTLY TAIL

Waterford City and County
Libraries

WULFIE

A GHOSTLY TAIL

Lindsay J Sedgwick

Illustrated by Rosa Devine

Little Island Books

WULFIE: A GHOSTLY TAIL

First published in 2022 by

Little Island Books

7 Kenilworth Park

Dublin 6W

Ireland

ISBN: 978-1-912417-84-1

Illustrated and designed by Rosa Devine
Edited by Venetia Gosling
Copy-edited and proofread by Emma Dunne

Printed in Poland by Skleniarz

· Little Island receives financial support from the Arts Council / An Chomhairle Ealaíon

10 9 8 7 6 5 4 3 2 1

For Ivy Rose, my granddaughter

Chapter 1

It was late afternoon. Weak sunlight spilled through the window as Libby carefully lifted a huge portrait down off the wall outside the bathroom. It was of a young woman with an enormous hairdo in the shape of a ship, complete with rigging and silken sails.

Wulfie reached up to help steady the picture's heavy gilt frame but shrank quickly back to medium-puppy size as Libby's stepmother, Veronika, stepped out of her bedroom onto the landing below.

'She looks just like you, Libby,' said Veronika, looking up and giving a short laugh. 'Stupid!'

'Oh,' said Libby and, 'thank you!' While she knew her stepmother had meant to insult her, the young woman in the frame *was* an ancestor, and Libby didn't think she looked stupid at all.

'You look happy.' Veronika waved a finger at Libby, her fingernails painted black with flames rising up them. 'It doesn't suit you.'

Libby forced herself to look sad and Veronika nodded. 'That's better.' She strode away downstairs, scratching a thumbnail along the colourful walls. 'The place looks better already without all their ugly mugs.'

The 'ugly mugs' were generations of Libby's ancestors who had hung on the walls all along the hall and up the four flights of stairs to Libby's attic room for as long as she could remember. She had talked to them as if they were friends, long before her real friend Wulfie had appeared from the trunk in her bedroom – a trunk that somehow also happened to be a portal to his wulfen world of Lupuslandia! The portrait currently in Libby's arms was of Catherine Mary Frances Flanagan, the only daughter of Libby's great-great-grandfather Zebediah, the owner of the trunk.

Libby felt an affinity with Catherine, since neither of them had been brought up by their mothers. The story was that the sea captain had returned home from an expedition to the South Seas with his young daughter, but no sign of her mum, while Libby's own mum had also been mislaid before Libby had turned two.

'Did you see that?' said Wulfie, once Veronika had turned the corner. 'She nearly smiled at me.'

'She wouldn't have and she never will,' said Libby and, 'Ssh!'

'Who are you ssh-ing?' Rex slithered out of his room, blocking Libby's path and separating her from Wulfie. 'The ghosts that are going to burst out of those ugly pictures the minute we're gone?'

Rex was Libby's not-so-adorable step-brother. She wished he wasn't.

He put down his overnight bag and grinned. 'Bet something scary comes out of that ugly trunk in your bedroom and gobbles you right up as soon as Mum and I have gone.'

Speaking of gobbling, Libby noticed that Wulfie was growing larger and hungrier behind her step-brother. Wulfie hated bullies, and when wulfens get angry, they grow enormous. Wulfie had already swallowed Rex once before for being mean to Libby, though only for a short time and just to teach him a lesson.

'NO!' she said to Wulfie, but Rex thought she meant it for him.

'No, you won't be scared, or no, you won't be eaten?' he said, grinning.

Rex's goal in life was to make Libby's life miserable. He was really very good at it most of the time, but Libby was too happy today to let him bother her. Humming to herself, she squeezed past him with the picture, whooshing Wulfie up the stairs ahead of her. Decorators were arriving tomorrow to paper the walls of the hall and stairwell, which was why Libby had been told to take all the pictures down.

Veronika had decided the upset and the wallpaper paste would be disastrous for her skin and hair and might give her darling Rexipoo headaches. To protect themselves, she and Libby's step-brother were moving into her sister Ilda's house until the decorators were done, Aunt Ilda being in jail for impersonating a dog and weeing on a policeman.

Among other things.

Therefore, for one entire day and two whole nights, Libby and Wulfie would be home alone with her dad. And as Dad would be tucked away in his Inventing Room most of the time, Wulfie would be able to relax and stop pretending to be a dog, at least once the decorators were finished for the day. He would be able to talk, and change shape, and throw furballs from his ears without anyone noticing him. It was going to be fun.

Which was why, despite knowing she'd miss the multi-coloured walls, right now Libby couldn't help but feel happier than a cup of cocoa full of melting marshmallows shaped like sleepy hedgehogs.

Rex was miffed, though. He didn't seem able to scare Libby any more, and she used to be terrified of his stories – even when he barely tried to make them frightening.

'The trunk will creak open at three minutes past midnight,' he said, following her up the stairs to her room. 'When the sky is completely dark, your room will be like a crypt and then this creature will emerge ...'

Libby pushed the door to her room open with her bum, her hands being full of ancestor.

'This creature will emerge ...' Rex repeated, kicking the door. 'It's maybe a skeleton or a wolf or—' Just inside the door, he stopped dead. The room was full of eyes.

Libby had decided that her room – though neither big nor warm – was a nicer place to store all her old friends than the cellar downstairs. The portraits were on the floor all around, leaning against the walls and staring at Rex. Uncomfortable, he focused on Libby, who was making space for the lady with the mad hair. 'You'll probably wee the bed too because if you put one foot on the floor, you'll be dragged by your toes into the trunk to be eaten alive by some weird dead animal come to life—'

'An animal like this?' Libby turned round to Rex and held a stuffed one-eyed rabbit on a redwood plinth out to him. It had come from Zebediah's trunk too and she'd named it Snuffles.

Not expecting this, her stepbrother stumbled back into a portrait of a cross-looking woman in a lace mantilla.

'You're more scared of the trunk than I am,' said Libby, smiling. The removal of the paintings had taken all afternoon, since Veronika had decided it was Libby's job to ready the house for the decorators, although she was only ten. Now that was done, she had no more chores to do, except to cover the hall floor and stairs with old sheets before the decorators came.

'Rexipoo!'

Veronika's voice was so sing-songy when she called her son and so sharp when Libby was the target. Not for the first time, Libby wondered how someone could be so nice to one child and so truly horrid to another. But then again, although they were both the same age, Rex was Veronika's son and, while Veronika insisted on Libby calling her Mum, she really wasn't like a mum to her at all.

Rex hesitated. Not being able to frighten Libby made him feel rotten inside.

It was all the fault of her dog, Rex decided. The dog made Libby braver, somehow. It was staring at him now, with eyes that Rex was sure shouldn't be yellow. Rex put his hand on the doorknob.

Something about Wulfie made him feel uncomfortable. Not afraid – he would never admit to fear – but as if he needed to keep his distance.

'That mutt better be nice to me,' he said, as Wulfie climbed off the trunk for a good stretch and yawned, revealing his sharp teeth deliberately.

'Time to go, sweetums!' Veronika was losing patience; her voice had a tiny tinge of maroon to it.

Rex turned and headed out of the door.

Libby and Wulfie listened to his footsteps on the stairs. Then they held their breath, waiting to hear the front door slam – Rex was almost as fond of slamming doors as he was of kicking them.

Slam!

They both grinned.

'So, what do you want to do first?' said Libby.

Chapter 2

First on the agenda was Wulfie growing to the size of a small wolf so he could feel the wind in his ears when he slid down the banister. Second was bouncing on Rex's bed while Libby tried out her step-brother's guitar.

For tea, Libby made pancakes, while Dad filled the table with toppings: from smelly cheese to chilli jam; from raspberry jelly and peanut butter to grated chocolate, pickles and marshmallows. Wulfie's nose gravitated towards the cheese, and Libby asked Dad if she could give him some.

'Never heard of a dog liking blue cheese,' said Dad. He squinted at Wulfie for a whole minute before stroking him behind the ears. 'But Wulfie isn't just any dog, is he?' That made Libby a bit nervous until he added, 'He's an intelligent creature. I would expect him to be a connoisseur of blue cheese – and he'd be doing me a favour. I bought far too much and Veronika says it makes my moustache curl.'

After eating the tiniest morsel of Dad's cheese, Wulfie smelt like honey mixed with golden syrup and melted marshmallows, which made everyone happy, the way nice smells can. Then, when Dad went back to his inventing, Libby and Wulfie took over the sitting room. Wulfie made himself as large as a small pony and nibbled on the cheese, while she lay against his stomachs and he introduced her to the sounds made by the creatures that digested his food for him.

Noisiest by far were the Spitglossums in stomach three. They sounded like wailing banshees, while the Mooshyguts in stomach two sounded exactly the way Libby imagined lava would sound bubbling out of a volcano. Then there were Smudgeeduns on the way from stomach two to stomach three. They whistled their way along, while the Whoofpoofkles between stomachs one and two made a sound very much like their name.

As far as Libby could tell, they all seemed to be very happy with the cheese, but the Stinky Sigusting-bugs in Wulfie's throat were the biggest surprise of all. With twenty-four legs each, they could sing a great many notes depending on how many legs they rubbed together. They were also the only digestive creature Wulfie had actually seen, although he had heard that Whoofpookles were long and thin, while Smudgeeduns were mostly nose.

Before Libby and Wulfie sat down to watch a film with Dad – about an inventor who accidentally turns his daughter into a possum and has to travel back in time to find a cure – Dad made Libby the thickest hot drink out of real chocolate and cream.

By the time Libby finally rolled into bed with Wulfie, she was feeling tired and full and warm.

'This is how home is *meant* to feel,' she said happily.

—

The next morning, Libby was still asleep when Wulfie dropped a mouthful of square biscuits on to her face. 'I got us breakfast!' he said. 'Your dad was baking and asked me if I'd like one, so I wagged my tail as if I was a dog and he put them on the floor for me.' Wulfie grinned, terribly proud of how dog-like he'd managed to be.

'Why don't you have them?' said Libby, since they all had an additional layer of wulfen drool on them, which definitely wasn't her favourite topping. Normally she had to make breakfast for Veronika and Rex first, and every-thing nice to eat ran out by the time she got to make her own. But today Libby only had to look after herself. She thought she might have French toast, and granola with yoghurt – and two types of fruit – and maybe Dad would make her another hot chocolate!

'The decorators have arrived,' said Wulfie.

'Did they see you?'

Wulfie nodded. 'But I was being a dog so I let them stroke me. Oh, and I was super careful going up and down the stairs so I wouldn't mess up the sheets you put down for them. Your dad made them a cup of tea to have in the kitchen before they start. They smell of sandwiches and toast.'

But Libby was hardly listening, having just thought of another thing she could only do when Rex and Veronika were away. She left Wulfie chewing – the biscuits were hard but they reminded him of the bread his mother baked for special wulfen festivals in Lupuslandia, so he was happy. Making herself walk slowly, Libby said goodbye to the coloured walls and the cracks in them that Dad called laughter lines as she made her way downstairs.

It was always wise to knock before going into Dad's Inventing Room at the top of the kitchen stairs. Libby remembered why when a sharp jet of water hit her between the eyes as she opened the door, knocking her onto her bum and sending her sliding back into the hall.

'Oops,' said Dad, turning the dial on a control panel and pointing the device at her again.

Before Libby could wipe her face, a blast of warm air – smelling vaguely of ginger – sucked all the water off her. Dad pulled her up onto her feet and into his room as the decorators came up from the kitchen to start papering the hall.

'Behold,' he said, once the door was shut behind her, 'the Master Blaster. The most powerful whoosher and de-whoosher yet!'

Libby recognised the base of Dad's new machine as the rocket Wulfie had designed for collecting rubbish. Now it was attached to an engine and a hose and had a complicated control panel with a dial – all painted green, her dad's favourite colour. (His jacket was green, and the walls of the Inventing Room were various shades of green, as were the tools spread across his two Inventing Desks and the Post-it notes and pens on his Thinking Desk by the wall.)

'Spin the dial to the picture of a trowel and it is pro-grammed to identify weeds, suck them up and spit them into this handy compostable pouch,' he said. 'Turn it to the picture of a plant, load up your seeds and it will plant them in exactly the pattern you choose. If you add the seeds one colour at a time, you could write a message in the flowerbed that you wouldn't be able to read until spring. Not that I've tested it yet, but I have high hopes!'

He turned the dial to the picture of a smiling face. From the back of the device, a slot opened and a latex ball emerged. As it inflated, Libby could see it was covered with fingers – like a sort of octopus with short knobbly legs – which began to vibrate. 'Prop the device on the back of your chair and give yourself a nice back massage after a hard day's planting,' said Dad. The ball blew off, landing on top of his bust of Marie Curie on the desk and deflating. 'It's not quite working yet but I'm also hoping to install a small music system so the machine will play a happy tune to encourage plants to grow and the sun to come out while the engine recharges.' He smiled shyly. 'I wanted to surprise your stepmother for our anniversary.'

'Wasn't she looking for a power hose?'

'Ah, that's this red button marked V. It's a jet strong enough to take the plaster off the outside walls, something Veronika seems very keen to do. I'm not sure it's a good idea, but she has such a way of talking and looking into your eyes that it then makes perfect sense.'

Libby had to say she didn't know this feeling. The only times Veronika looked into Libby's eyes, she was cross or trying to scare her. Sometimes it seemed to Libby that her stepmother was three different people – to herself, to Rex and to Dad – and that Libby got the worst of them. But right now, what did it matter? Libby had the house to herself!

'Can Nazim come over?'

Nazim was the first school friend Libby had made that Rex hadn't scared off, and his dog, Zodiac, was Wulfie's biggest fan.

'Excellent idea,' said Dad, ringing Nazim's parents immediately. He'd be working on his Master Blaster and other devices all day, including an attachment for Veronika's headphones that would allow her to eliminate absolutely all background noise, so it would be good for Libby to have company.

Fortunately, Nazim's parents thought it would be good for Nazim to have company too, since they were both working.

Dad ended the call and smiled at his daughter. 'He'll be here in half an hour. Why don't you buy some treats for yourself and Nazim while you wait?' he said, giving her a jumble of coins from his pocket.

Having a friend over was a huge thing for Libby. She had never been able to have anyone round before. Veronika would have objected to Libby being distracted from chores, while Rex, well, Rex would have just been mean.

As she was leaving the room, Dad handed her a tin of the biscuits he'd baked. 'Bit too hard for my teeth, or yours,' he said, 'but Wulfie seems to like them. Tell him they're a gift from me so he won't eat the treats you get for yourself and your friend!'

Libby said hello to the decorators on her way out the front door, before speeding down the road with Wulfie to the corner shop.

She had decided that she and Nazim would picnic up on the roof.

Chapter 3

'So *this* is the famous trunk,' said Nazim, running his hand along the leather straps. 'It looks so *ordinary*!'

Libby nodded and unlocked the catch.

'I mean, it's an awesome trunk because it's so old – but it doesn't look like a portal to another world.'

'You can look inside if you like.'

His hand on the latch, Nazim hesitated. 'I won't be sucked into Lupuslandia?'

'The portal hasn't opened since Wulfie arrived,' said Libby. 'As far as we know.' She stroked Wulfie between the ears. She knew he got homesick sometimes. It couldn't be easy for him, not knowing if he'd ever see his mum again – something they had in common.

'I know this!' Nazim pulled out the red velvet cape. 'Wulfie wore this when he was being WonderWulf and saving the world! Oh, but these are cool.'

'These' were a pair of black boots with toes that curled up. Next Nazim found a pair of baggy trousers with patches and pockets, a shirt with ruffles, a hat with broken peacock feathers and the largest roll of silk ribbon. 'You could circle the house with it twice!' he said. 'Silk's meant to be really strong. Maybe Zebediah bought it to sell?'

Every time Zebediah's trunk opened, there were new things to find. Nazim's next discovery was a bottle with a ship inside that his pug Zodiac found mesmerising. Then he pulled out a single velvet glove – green – and a glittery lace mantilla wrapped around a wooden peg doll, while Wulfie found a patchwork waistcoat, embroidered with gold thread, and a watch-chain. Libby was delighted to see that it fitted the odd device her dad had given her – the watch-that-wasn't-only-a-watch and that only ticked when Wulfie wasn't well.

Libby was still surprised by what came out of Zebediah's trunk – not having had the longest time to get used to having a magical trunk in her room, let alone an adorable wulfen friend on whose nose Nazim had just draped a bridle made of sea pearls.

Wulfie offered it to Zodiac, who lowered her head so that Wulfie could slip it on. Then she twirled and twirled until she was dizzy, finally stopping and flopping down on the tattered rug beside Libby's bed.

'That waistcoat is his,' said Nazim, pointing at a man in one of the paintings around Libby's room. 'And this,' he said, draping the lace mantilla over his head, 'looks a bit like hers. Which one of them is Zebediah?'

'None of them,' said Libby.

'You'd have thought he'd have been painted, him being a sea captain with a beard you could hide a piano inside,' said Nazim with a grin, 'according to your dad!'

'Dad said I used to talk to Zebediah when I was tiny,' said Libby, thinking the peg doll looked somehow familiar. 'I'd be chatting away but there'd be no-one there, and when Mum or Dad asked who I was talking to, I'd say "Bed-iah".'

'Awesome,' said Nazim. 'Like an invisible friend who's a ghost!'

'What's a ghost?' asked Wulfie.

Libby had to think how to explain it. She didn't want him to be scared. 'A ghost is the spirit of someone who's died,' she said. 'Sometimes they miss the people they love so much that they want to still visit them. Or they have some kind of unfinished business they want to come back and sort out. But not everyone believes in them, and I've never seen one.

'I think this was his ship,' she said, picking up her favourite painting. It was of a tall ship in full sail sitting high on the water, all rigging and billowing sails. 'Dad says that Zebediah could speak any language within minutes!'

'Wonder if he knew his trunk was a portal,' said Nazim. 'I mean, he must have, right? Since it was his trunk.'

Libby shrugged. 'I didn't until Wulfie appeared. If it had never been opened at the right time before, maybe no-one did?'

Once they had dressed up like every one of her ancestors in the paintings, they fetched the sandwiches she'd made earlier and took them back to her room to add to the treats she'd bought. 'Want to eat up on the roof?' said Libby.

Nazim grinned. 'Can we?'

Libby nodded to Wulfie. He grew big enough to nose open the skylight. A few seagulls objected to being disturbed, but since they didn't fancy being eaten by a large purple wulfen, they flew off to a nearby pier to pester tourists for chips instead.

First Wulfie lifted Libby up, with her WonderWulf knapsack of food and the rug from beside her bed, then Nazim. Zodiac told Wulfie with a series of undulating barks and a couple of bum wiggles that she was not, under any circumstance, going up through any hole in a ceiling. Instead, she settled down on Libby's bed to chew on some dog treats and daydream about sticks, while Wulfie went up to join the two friends.

Between the eaves, there was a nice flat space, sheltered from the wind, where Libby laid out the rug. She unpacked the food she'd brought, to which Nazim added pouches of his mum's samosas and bhajis and pakora and a bottle of pink fizzy stuff that they drank too fast and which sent bubbles up their noses.

'The wall outside the bathroom was that colour,' said Libby, pointing at the bottle, as she tried to describe how colourful the house had been before the decorators had started work. 'But the hall walls were the best. The bottom halves were green on one side and blue on the other, with pumpkin and papaya stripes above. You could see the colours through the glass in the front door if you put your nose to it.'

'We never redecorate,' said Nazim, 'since we don't know how long each of Mum's postings will last. She could be sent anywhere – she says that's the great thing about working for the diplomatic service, but I'm not sure. This time I'd kind of like to stay put.'

They looked out across the rooftops, past the roadworks at the end of the street and into the park. There was a shopping centre on the far side, but after Wulfie's adventure there, when he'd foiled some thieves and accidentally been gassed, Libby was trying to avoid it for a while.

It was cold and a little bit windy up on the roof, so Wulfie fetched their coats and scarves and the old hat with feathers to keep Libby's head warm. 'It's like being on board a ship,' said Nazim. He tied his scarf to a thin pipe that stuck up through the roof for no apparent reason. The breeze made it flap briefly. 'That's our pirate flag, our skull and crossbones. And if we had a plank to walk, it'd be there. You'd land on the bathroom roof, though, and probably be fine.'

Libby looked around at the low scudding clouds and sky. They could be at sea.

Nazim placed his hands on a pretend wheel behind the chimney stack, as if he was standing at the helm of a boat. 'Now, where would you like to go, Captain?'

Libby gave him her hat with the broken feathers – it was a Captain-y sort of hat – and looked at Wulfie. 'First Mate?'

Wulfie frowned. He wasn't a fan of water. Water made him shrink even when he didn't want to, but maybe ... since it was all imagining ... 'Home?'

Libby wrapped her arms around him. 'Set a course for Lupuslandia!' she said.

—

Nazim had to be back for a family dinner, so just before six he and Libby said goodbye, and Wulfie lifted a paw to Zodiac as she bounded down the front steps. The decorators finished up shortly after, so while Dad cooked, Libby laid the kitchen table properly. It was like old times, before Veronika had insisted he give up baking, since she was better at it, and focus on inventing things that would make them rich.

By the time Dad served up, the kitchen smelt delicious, as if you could eat it all up, and every mouthful of his pie made Libby feel warm and happy inside. He'd even baked a sniffy little pie for Wulfie, who sat up at the table and ate very daintily – while still pretending to be a dog, so he couldn't use his paws.

'I'm working through that old recipe book of Zebediah's,' said Dad. 'This is called The Happiness Pie. Strange name but, even odder, we had all the ingredients needed – though I did add a few of my own.'

Dad couldn't help doing a bit of inventing, even with food.

'There were stains all over the page,' he added. 'So I'm guessing it was one of Zebediah's favourites.'

'Is that where the biscuits came from too?'

He nodded.

'The Happiness Pie is better,' said Libby. 'Though maybe you didn't need to add grapefruit segments as well as chilli peppers?'

—

Libby was determined to wake early the next day so she and Wulfie could have breakfast together downstairs before Veronika and Rex returned, so Wulfie sang her a wulfen lullaby to help her get to sleep quickly. Unusually for a lullaby, it was all about war. Luckily Libby didn't understand Lupuslandian, which has lots of words that sound like clicking and tapping, so she fell soundly asleep and dreamt she was the world's greatest flamenco dancer.

But it must have been a very powerful lullaby because neither she nor Wulfie woke up until the whole house was full of sunlight the following day.

Libby opened her bedroom door and rubbed her eyes. Now that all the walls had been papered, leaving her room in daylight was like stepping out into a beige pencil case. No home should look like the inside of a pencil case, and no pencil case should ever be beige. They should be made of pink and purple fur, or covered with drawings of wolves and magical beasts.

Or at least look like an ice-cream sundae.

'It doesn't feel like my home today,' she said sadly.

'The coloured walls are still there,' said Wulfie. 'Underneath.'

If Libby and Wulfie had been up on the roof in their 'pirate ship', they would have seen Veronika's car turn in to Longish Strand Road. It was travelling at speed and ignored the Stop sign at the roadworks, forcing the workmen present – both called Fred – to dive into the bottom of the hole they'd just dug.

But Libby and Wulfie were already on their way downstairs, Libby looking at her feet rather than the walls so she could pretend the bright colours were still there. Before she reached the bathroom floor, Wulfie grew huge as a pony, plucked Libby up onto his back and gallop–slid the rest of the way downstairs. Holding tight to his muzzle, Libby laughed with joy and forgot all about the walls.

'This is the only way to travel!' she shouted.

They landed in a muddle of dusty decorators' sheets at the bottom of the stairs, just as Veronika slid her key into the front-door lock.

'Quick, shrink!' said Libby.

Wulfie immediately shrank to the dog size Veronika would expect to see, his favourite one of medium-sized puppy, and vanished under the tangle of sheets.

As the door opened, Libby scooped the sheets up with Wulfie inside.

'Just cleaning up,' she said to Veronika, stifling a giggle and heading for the washing machine.

Chapter 4

Vacuuming one floor at a time, Libby unplugged the hoover and moved it up from one landing to the next while Wulfie kept his distance. He'd nearly had his tail sucked up once.

'Can we go to the park when you've hoovered?' he asked when they were safely past Rex's room.

'*Sssh*,' said Libby. 'I still have to mop the stairs and bathroom after this.'

When she reached the next floor, Wulfie was sitting there with his legs crossed tightly.

'Don't!' said Libby, turning off the hoover. 'Dogs can't sit like that.'

So Wulfie stood and hopped from foot to foot, the

way he'd seen Libby do when she was desperate for the loo.

'Or that!'

Wulfie pleaded with his biggest eyes.

'Can't you wait till we go to the park?' said Libby. Wulfie shook his head. She caught the small purple furball that flew out of his left ear and put it in her pocket. 'Seriously?'

Rex had been playing his guitar in his room since his return. Veronika was napping. She had bought head-phones the day after she'd bought Rex his electric guitar, when she'd realised how bad his playing actually was. It had been very bad. Like cars being ground down into pencil shavings. This meant that they were both safely in their rooms.

'Okay,' Libby said. 'I'll let you out into the garden for a wee but remember: no talking or growing.'

'Because I'm a dog.'

'*Ssh.*'

Wulfie trotted ahead of her down the stairs. His tail was high and wagging, his bum wiggling as he took the tall stairs one at a time. Libby had thought she could never love him more but every so often, well, she just did. 'One wee only,' she said, leaving the back door ajar. 'And come straight back to me the minute you see Veronika or Rex.'

Wulfie nodded, only half-hearing as his nose dragged him towards a peeing spot that smelt of cats and pigeons: the sort of smell no four-legged creature of wulfen stock could ignore.

Libby watched him track the scent to the hedge they shared with their neighbour, Mr H, his boyfriend and their thirteen cats. Wulfie looked like a tiny purple wolf, ears up and tail flat to the ground.

Several floors above, Rex was trying out his latest lyrics.

'My scaredy-cat step-sister
Is just like a blister;
If the dog was gone
She'd be scared of this song!'

Rex was already bored. His song wasn't as awesome as he'd expected it to be. Then he looked outside, spotted Wulfie and grinned.

If Wulfie was outside, then Libby was alone!

—

Having put the hoover away, Libby fetched the mop, filled the bucket and began walking backwards up the kitchen stairs and along the hall, mopping the wooden floor as she went. Normally she stayed with Wulfie when he went outside, to make sure nothing happened, but with Rex and Veronika in their rooms, he was probably safer away from her bucket of water.

She was nearly at the landing above Rex's room and the bathroom when something landed in her hair. It wriggled like a hand and tangled in her curls. Libby jumped, jolting the mop, which tipped the bucket of water back down the steps into the hall.

Sniggers erupted from the banister on the top floor. Rex was laughing so hard, he thought he might wet himself. He pulled the spider – a rubber-legged toy tarantula – back up on its elastic. 'Priceless,' he said, coming down the stairs towards her. Libby stepped quickly out of his way into the bathroom. 'Oh, Mum says not to put the Uglies up again.'

'Why not?' Libby had been looking forward to hanging her ancestors' portraits back up – it seemed the only way to put some colour back on the walls.

'She says they'll put people off.'

'What people?' said Libby, wishing the paintings had put Veronika off marrying her dad five years earlier.

Rex smiled. His mum had told him why she was redecorating. It was meant to be a secret until everything was settled, but keeping secrets was boring. And hard! 'I'll miss this house,' he said, stepping over Libby's mop, before changing his mind and kicking it downstairs.

Libby felt her heart race as Rex made footprints in the water and splashed the new beige walls. *Were Veronika and Rex moving out? Maybe that was why they'd been over at Aunt Ilda's house, not just to avoid the decorators?*

'I'm sure the house won't miss you,' she said, feeling brave all over.

'Or you, either.' Rex's voice took on a sneer all of its own, a racing-car sneer full of speed and sleekness. 'We're selling this stupid house ...'

Chapter 5

Rex droned on while Libby fetched the bucket and started mopping up the spilt water. He followed her all the way downstairs, saying something about having a bigger bedroom and a garage for his band to practise in. Not getting any response from Libby, he lost interest and headed back up to his room to dig into the stash of treats he'd stolen from his aunt's house.

Libby wasn't listening to him because she was desperately trying to think.

Rex wanted to scare her. That was all. Everyone knew she loved this house, especially her tiny attic bedroom. Unable to scare her with stories about monsters, Rex must have decided to move on to her deeper fears instead. Libby was even a little impressed—

Except ... Her step-brother wasn't that smart.

'He's trying to make me forget to do my chores so that I get into trouble with Veronika,' she decided, and mopped the steps right to the top of the house before she let herself start thinking again. Then she carried the mop and bucket downstairs and emptied the water down the sink in the laundry room before traipsing back to her room.

Where she sat on the trunk and tried to work out what Rex had meant.

Her ancestors looked up at her, unblinking, as she counted to ten upwards and backwards and tried not to panic. The Flanagan family had always lived here. Long before Zebediah's father had built this house, there had been a cottage on this very spot for generations of Flanagans. It was from this very house that her great-great-grandfather had headed off to sea, before returning to make it a home for himself and his daughter, and adding the top two floors.

Libby couldn't imagine living anywhere else.

She didn't want to.

It had to be a mistake. Dad would never let the house be sold – would he?

—

Before Libby could get to Dad's Inventing Room to ask him, Veronika, beautifully rested from her nap, summoned Libby into the sitting room and handed her a measuring tape to hold while she walked with the other end of it to the far side of the dining table. Veronika wrote the dimensions down in a little black book, then let go of her end of the measuring tape. It snapped back into Libby's hand like a sharp-sided snake.

'Have you mopped the stairs?'

Libby nodded.

'Good.' Veronika took the measuring tape back from her. 'When they're dry, you can polish them, but for now, go and make me a nice cup of coffee. With froth.'

'Dad will never let you!' Libby burst out.

'Let me what?'

'Sell the house,' said Libby.

Veronika thought about lying but lies were tedious things. She knew she would need Libby to keep the house clean until it sold, but the temptation to be mean overwhelmed common sense. Veronika showed Libby the book she'd been reading: *Tips for Making Everyone Want to Pay FAR Too Much for Your Crummy Old House.* 'It's so easy to transform even an ugly house like this into something someone will want to buy,' she said. 'Though they'll probably rip out all the walls and paint the place white.'

'It's not an ugly house,' said Libby.

Veronika ignored her, if she heard her at all. 'On the other hand, "character" can increase the price enormously. Ghosts, for example. Also ancient murders, millionaires gone mad – we haven't any of those, have we?'

Libby shook her head.

'Pity. Still, I've done all I can. That ridiculous colour scheme is gone and the pictures are ready for the skip. Three leading estate agents are coming to value the house next week. A hefty asking price will make it easier for your father, who is oddly attached to this misshapen place ...'

Libby backed towards the door as Veronika turned away.

'No ghosts in your crummy little attic, are there?' said her stepmother. 'It's such a creepy room. There's bound to be a spooky something hiding in that stupid old trunk or living within the walls. Well?'

She spun round – but Libby was already gone.

—

Dad's *Enter All Who Questions Ask* sign was missing from his Inventing Room door, and the door itself had been painted white and glossy, as if it had never had a smudgy fingerprint or a nudge of Wulfie's nose on it. Libby remembered to knock but forgot to wait for Dad to answer, and this time a delicate jet of cobwebs landed on her nose.

'Oops!' Dad pressed a switch on his latest gadget and sucked the cobweb back in. 'Sorry! Used to be a water pistol. Now it's a De-web Webber and a Re-web Webber. Spiders don't have to lose their webs any more. We suck them up and fire them into a hedge outside.'

Libby's height had been measured on the inside of Dad's door, and that had been painted over too. Flat-pack boxes were lined up against the wall, waiting to be filled.

'Time for a bit of a tidy up, apparently,' he said when he saw Libby looking at them.

'Dad, how can you let Veronika sell our house?'

'Ah.' Dad laid his latest device down on one of his Inventing Desks, alongside the sign from the door. 'I was hoping she'd lose interest.' He looked around the room – at every corner, every shelf, every crumb, every box of bits and bobs, and nuts and bolts.

Libby knew he loved this house as much as she did.

His eyes fell to the desk. 'It's so very hard to say no to her when she turns her big green eyes on me, the way you know she can ...'

Libby didn't know. Veronika never, *ever* looked at Libby in any way that made Libby feel wanted or intriguing or interesting at all. 'But this is the best house anyone could ever live in!' Since she hadn't phrased it as a question, her dad didn't hear it or reply. She started again: 'Dad, isn't this our home? Yours and mine and even Zebediah's? And,' she said quietly, 'my mum's?'

Dad deflated onto his chair and sighed, all oomph gone from him like a balloon with a slow puncture. 'Veronika says it would be better for us as a family to live closer together, not spread throughout a big tall house. She thinks that a warm modern house would be healthier overall.'

'Can't you stop her, Dad? Say you made a mistake?'

He fumbled with the papers on his desk. 'If my inventions made a bit more money, we could make the house more comfortable. I did promise her a mansion, carpet on the stairs ...' Dad stopped talking. Libby looked so small and sad and he wanted to make her happy too. 'Perhaps I could rig up my fartometer to go off regularly when she has people in to view. Or we could make faces at the window? Hide behind doors?'

Libby shrugged, trying to smile. She was pretty certain Veronika would make sure they were both far away from the house whenever she had buyers booked in. Dad knew it too. Libby suddenly got a bad feeling. The sort that's like a tummy ache, with icy fingers writing '*Uh-oh*' on your back. There was something missing from the room.

'Dad?' she said. 'Where's the Master Blaster?'

'Oh, I asked Rex to take it outside,' said Dad, 'to charge it up in the shed.'

Wulfie was outside. And now Rex was outside too, with a hatred for her wulfen friend and armed with a machine that could blast plaster from walls!

Libby rushed from the room.

Chapter 6

Hardly daring to breathe, Libby tore down the stairs into the kitchen, skidded into the laundry room and dashed out through the back door. Wulfie was sniffing around in some bushes near the end of the garden. Birds were singing, and there was no sign of Rex or the Master Blaster.

She sighed with relief. 'Wulfie!'

Wulfie's tail went up when he saw her but he neither said 'hi' nor raised a thumb, because he was meant to be a dog. Instead, he trotted towards her, wagging his tail, and Libby relaxed. He was on his way back, safe and sound ... when Rex stepped out of the shed. He was wearing his Iron Man helmet, and Dad's Master Blaster sat against his shoulder like the weapon it was – if you were small or leafy or dirt of any kind.

'Wulfie,' said Libby. 'Come here!'

'No. No. *No!*' Veronika stormed out of the house behind Libby, bee-lining directly for her son. 'That thing is far too dangerous for you to use.'

O-kay, thought Libby. Not whom she'd expect to save Wulfie, but she would take it. 'Come on, Wulfie,' she said as Veronika demanded the Master Blaster from her son, who looked furious. 'Let's go inside.'

Wulfie looked from her to Veronika and altered course.

'Wulfie!' Libby shouted. 'I said *inside*. Now!'

Despite everything Libby had said to him,

Wulfie clung obstinately to the misguided idea that he could make Libby's stepmother love him, and not only because he was as cute as a fluffy purple carpet monster with a tail. Libby knew this was impossible. Veronika thought *Rex* was adorable – her sense of who was worth liking was not the same as anyone else's.

Besides, her step-mother hated any-thing with four legs and fur.

And she hated Wulfie more than all of them because every time she wanted to get rid

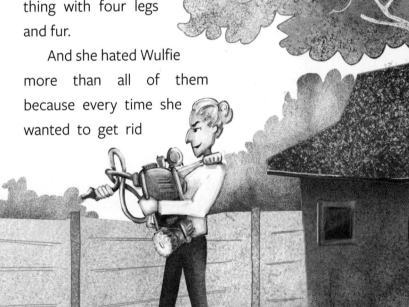

of him, something got in the way, such as him becoming the model for a nationwide eco-superhero or delight-fully embarrassing her sister live on national TV.

Libby saw Veronika brace her legs, assassin-style, and knew she was powerless to stop what her stepmother was about to do.

'Hello, doggy,' said Veronika.

Wulfie glanced back at Libby, as if to say, *Told you*.

Veronika turned the dial on the Master Blaster to the red button. 'Fancy a clean?'

'Veronika – *Mum*, no!'

'I beg your pardon?' said Veronika, treating Libby to a stare powerful enough to bring down spy satellites.

'The hose,' said Libby. 'That setting, it's too strong. You'll hurt him.'

'What? *This* little button?' Her stepmother moved her eyebrows into what was meant to be an innocent frown.

'I'll wash him properly,' said Libby, pleading now. 'I promise!'

Veronika's mouth stretched into what could have been a grin, if grins meant certain death to those treated to one, and she pressed the button. The water came out at such speed and with such strength that Veronika was forced backwards towards the wall of the shed.

Left and right the hose spun, up and down, battering the garden, the hedge, taking plaster off the back wall and washing half the flowerbed towards the outside drain. Libby sped into the shed and unplugged the flex but by then the Master Blaster had cleared half the grass, most of the path and exposed a section of wooden beams built into the back wall of the house.

'There,' said Veronika. 'Much tidier.'

'I could have done that better,' said Rex, scowling.

'Wulfie?' Libby spun round and round, her eyes scanning every blade of grass. Wulfie shrank when he was wet, and now there was no sign of him anywhere.

Veronika frowned. 'That dog moves too fast. I don't like dogs who move fast. They might creep up on me.'

Libby couldn't reply. She was following the streams of water down the remains of the path to where they rushed full pelt into ... the drain.

'If I've scared him off, all well and good,' said Veronika, unwinding herself from the flex. 'Your fault for not keeping the mutt under control.'

Libby didn't react. It felt as if all the bones in her body had turned to dust, just like that.

Her best friend.

In the whole world.

Down the drain.

'He only wanted you to like him,' she said, staring down at the muddy water gurgling through the grid.

'He's hardly down there, idiot child,' said Veronika. 'Now, haven't you got chores to do? I can blast you too, you know. That would tidy up the house no end!'

Rex sniggered.

Before Veronika was tempted to turn the Master Blaster on her step-daughter, Libby's dad pottered out of the kitchen and into the garden. He sort-of-accidentally stood between his daughter and Veronika before remembering why he'd come outside in the first place and turning right to put his tea-bags in the compost bin under the kitchen window. (They were green tea and ginger, smells Veronika couldn't abide, so they had to go outside immediately after use.)

Veronika handed him the Master Blaster. 'I'd ask you not to give such a dangerous device to my sensitive son,' she said, heading inside with Rex. 'He might have hurt himself.'

As soon as Dad had followed them back into the kitchen, Libby called Wulfie's name down into the drain as loudly as she could. 'Wulfie, please come back. Don't get washed away.'

She'd been so worried about the house being sold that she'd forgotten about him being outside. 'I should have scooped you up as soon as I saw you,' she said, her heart heavy. 'I should have taken you for a walk when you needed to go.'

Today was really turning out to be the rottenest, nastiest, yuckiest day ever.

Chapter 7

One minute Wulfie had been trotting towards Veronika, his tail in the air. The next he was walloped by water so cold and so hard that he immediately shrank. By the time the water reached the grate, he was teeny tiny and was swept down into the drain, along the pipe running under the house and into the water main that ran down the road.

As Libby called his name, the tiny wulfen came to a halt upside down and back to front. His bum had collided with a solid, fatty lump of smelly stuff that was blocking the main. Hungry from all the whooshing and bumping about, Wulfie decided a nibble of something this stinky would make him feel better and stronger, so he might be able push back against the water building up behind him.

He ate a little and then a little more, burrowing in until he was pretty much stuck in the middle of the mound, with a ton of water behind him and no way forward or back.

—

In the deep hole dug into the tail end of Longish Strand Road, the two workmen called Fred had decided the best way to deal with whatever was blocking the main was to break it up by poking it. So the Fred who was whiskery and liked reciting poetry backwards in his sleep inserted a special sort of rod and, well, poked.

This blockage, however, made a sound suspiciously like an *ouch* and then an *oops*, because Wulfie knew he wasn't meant to be caught speaking aloud by anyone except Libby and Nazim. Puzzled, the Freds removed their poking rod, fed a camera into the pipe instead and peered into the gloom.

They saw a long purple snout and two yellow eyes staring back at them.

Before you could say 'What big eyes you've got', Whiskery Fred pulled the camera out and his partner inserted the top of their most powerful hose. Seconds later, Wulfie and the remains of the blockage were catapulted backwards down the pipe.

Towards and past Libby's house.

'Right …' said the Freds, climbing out of the hole and heading for the nearest café. When you heard voices coming from a drain and saw spooky yellow eyes, it was time for chocolate cake.

—

Poor Wulfie! It was like running a marathon backwards in a very wet fur suit. He scrabbled to find a hold but to no avail. Fortunately, the flow he was in met water emptying from the washing machine in number 18, six doors up from Libby's house.

When the two opposing streams met, Wulfie was shunted sideways into a (temporarily) dry pipe.

—

Upstairs in Libby's house, Veronika put her *Do Not Disturb* sign on the bedroom door and pulled out her laptop to tune in to reruns of her favourite TV show, *Most Horribly Haunted Houses*. Seeing other people scared witless was funny to her. It was also the only way she knew to truly relax since her other favourite show, *Playing Truly Mean and Nasty Pranks on Your Family*, had been cancelled.

Secretly, Veronika was a little bit jealous of the people featured on the TV show. Even her sister Ilda had seen a ghost, as had her mother and several of her aunts, but Veronika never had.

Not once. Not ever.

She'd hardly even had goosebumps.

Veronika turned her headphones to the new Cancel Every Noise setting that Dad had added, so that nothing would disturb her, and settled down to enjoy the show.

—

Libby sat by the back wall, barely noticing the water seeping through her jeans. What if Wulfie had shrunk small enough to be swept away into a huge reservoir? Or out to sea where he might be eaten by fish the size of dragons?

'Oh, Wulfie, I'm sorry I didn't take you for a walk, and I'm sorry about the hose.' She didn't know if he could hear her, if he was nearby or even if her voice would carry down into the drains, but she had to try. She kept checking Zebediah's watch-that-wasn't-only-a-watch. It had started ticking the last time when Wulfie was ill, and it had stopped again when he got better.

If it isn't ticking now, that has to mean he's okay, she thought. *Doesn't it?*

'You're more important than this house, Wulfie,' she said. 'You're more important than anything.'

—

Shaking himself dry, Wulfie fired a couple of small sodden furballs out of his left ear. Now dry, he was able to grow a bit bigger and felt a bit braver, so he decided to follow the pipe he was in. It was heading away from the road, and that was in the direction of Libby's home. As he went, he told himself about the smelly socks Libby would find for him when they saw each other again and the cuddles they'd have, how they'd laugh about him surfing on waves beneath the road, as if it wasn't scary and dark ...

Fortunately, wulfens have excellent night vision, so they can see in the dark. But when all you can see is more dark, even if you are the bravest wulfen in the world, night vision doesn't really help. So it was around this time that a strange noise was heard echoing up through the pipes and into numbers 15 and 16 Longish Strand Road as a small wulfen hummed loudly to keep himself company.

When the pipe turned upwards, Wulfie knew it wasn't leading to Libby's back garden. Still, he flexed his paws against the side of the pipe and started to climb. Libby's room was upwards, so up – he reckoned – was better than down.

Or so he thought, until the owner of number 16 let out the water from her morning bath. The wulfen smelt it coming, an overload of persimmon and orchid and glitter, but the force of the water still took him by surprise. It tumbled him back down and into the main before one claw found a join in the pipes.

Then, like a wet purple flag, Wulfie held on as all the water whooshed past before taking another deep breath and heading back along the main. He was feeling for pipes that led sideways and away from the road, hoping that the next one he tried would lead him home.

In number 10, three doors down from Libby's house, Wulfie was flushed out by an overloaded dishwasher, and in number 12 – Mr H's house – by water full of cat fur, as Mr H and his partner, Ed, washed two of their pets in the sink. By then Wulfie recognised the sound of water coming. He would tuck the tip of his tail into his mouth and brace all four paws on either side of the pipe so the water would flow under him, as if he were a furry sort of bridge.

But Wulfie was tired and his paws were sore. He was missing Libby and he didn't like the dark. So when the water had passed this last time, he lowered himself back down and howled.

He howled as loud as he could, from the bottom of his lungs, because he was lost and he wanted to be found.

Because he didn't know what to do next.

Because he was scared he'd never get home.

Chapter 8

Wulfie's howl fled left and right and sideways into all the pipes of all the houses up and down the street. Several dogs howled back, and two men noticed the vibrations in the water as they washed up after lunch. One little child who was deaf felt the vibrations in the wall and clapped her hands for the first time.

But one ten-year-old girl leapt to her feet and wiped her eyes.

'The pipes!' Libby cried. 'He's in the pipes! WULFIE!' she shouted down the drain. 'I love you so much. Hold on! I *will* get you out.'

She ran into Dad's Inventing Room without knocking, but remembered to duck, just in case. Seeing Libby, Dad wanted to tell her that she was right about the house but before he could speak—

'The pipes and the drains,' she said. 'How do they work?'

'Well, water goes down and through them and—'

'No, I mean—' Libby tried to work out what she wanted to ask exactly. 'If something went down the drain outside our house, could it climb back up?'

'Well ...' Dad began rooting through papers on his desk. 'Rats have been known to make their way up from the drains into houses ... Provided nobody turned the taps on ...'

'And if they did?'

'Back down into the main, I'm afraid. Start all over. Like a slippery game of snakes and ladders.' He found what he was looking for and put it on the desk in front of her. It seemed to be a plan of the house but with all its structural work exposed – waste pipes, supply pipes, the electrical wiring.

'Veronika needed to see the house plans and I found these with them, but see here.' He pointed to a blue line that wriggled alongside the walls of the stairwell. 'This pipework dates from the 1840s and isn't used now, but to avoid it, most of the pipes in the house do completely irrational detours – which might explain why our water pressure is so poor. Other pipes, like this one that ends in the wall behind Rex's room, don't even lead anywhere. They just stop for no reason at all, as if whoever put them in forgot why.'

Libby realised that the longer Wulfie was in the pipe system, the greater the chance of him getting washed away. She had to find a way to direct him back to the right house. Then he'd be able to shrink small enough to squeeze out of a plughole.

She would flavour the water so Wulfie would know which house was theirs!

'Dad, where does the water we use come from?'

—

Libby pulled open the crawl door at the end of the corridor beside her attic room. There was just enough attic left for the water tank, and it sat like a block of black ice by the end wall. Crouching over the tank, she pulled her sleeves over her hands and heaved until the lid shifted.

Once there was a gap, she crumbled a handful of Dad's smelly cheese into the cold, deep water.

In case that wasn't enough to contaminate the house's whole water supply, she added two socks from the laundry basket and a vest from Rex's sports bag. Then she closed the crawl door behind her and ran quietly down all four flights of stairs and down another flight to the kitchen and closed the door behind her.

Leaning over the kitchen sink, which had the lowest plug hole in the house, Libby called down, hoping her voice would echo through the pipes and reach her friend. 'Wulfie, it's me.' Her voice sounded tinny. 'I've made our water stinky – so you can find your way home.' She ran a tiny bit of water so Wulfie would smell it. 'Howl if you can hear me.'

Libby put the house plans on the draining board with the watch-that-wasn't on top and told Wulfie how much she missed him. That he had to come home and she'd never leave him alone again. She kept talking because it was the best thing she could think of to do.

Under the road, five doors down, Wulfie heard an echo of his best friend's voice, because wulfen ears are

very finely tuned. He turned towards the sound, moving quickly, finally catching the scent of smelly socks and stinky cheese.

It was faint, but enough to make him run as fast as he could – like a snail trail leading him home.

Just when Libby was feeling hopeless, the faintest howl echoed up through the plughole. 'Wulfie?' She tapped the sink so he'd hear the sound. 'Wulfie? This way!'

Seconds later, she heard his voice. 'Libby?' It sounded small and echoey and a long way away.

She tried to peer down the plughole. 'This way, Wulfie. You're nearly there!'

And he was – running as fast as he could, his foot-steps coming closer and closer until they stopped. He was stuck in the U-bend under the sink. 'I can't move,' he said. 'Can you get me out?'

'Can't you shrink teeny tiny?' said Libby. 'Like the time you hid in my ear?'

To her horror, Wulfie began to sob. It was the saddest sound Libby had ever heard. She wanted to rip out the sink and grab her best friend. 'I'm too tired to control how I grow or shrink,' he said, trying not to cry any more. 'I've gone round and round and I keep getting soaked – and it's so dark.'

Libby studied the plans on the draining board. She traced her finger along the pipes to a long straight line that led to the roof: the venting pipe. The pipe that Nazim had tied his scarf around.

'It's okay,' she said. 'There's another way out.'

Libby crumbled the last bit of cheese down the plughole and ran the tiniest bit of water so it would reach her friend. As he ate, she described the route he needed to take, initially to reach the bathroom. 'Once you're there, you'll find a pipe on the right that leads to the roof. I'll tap the walls near the pipes as much as I can, so you know I'm here.'

'I miss you,' he said.

'I miss you too,' said Libby.

'Talking to a sink now. That's funny,' said Rex, striding into the room. 'Funny stupid!' He pushed her away and filled a glass of water from the tap.

Wulfie heard him and growled.

Rex dropped his glass and jumped back from the sink. 'What was that?'

'I didn't hear anything,' said Libby, running out and up the stairs into the hall, tapping the walls as she went. 'Maybe *you* were talking to yourself?'

Chapter 9

Veronika paused the TV show on her laptop and slid off her bed to stand in front of her full-length mirror. Of all the special equipment the presenters used to hunt ghosts on her favourite show, the heat-sensing cameras were her favourite, though she loved the blurred night-vision shots too, especially the way they would hold the camera on someone's face to film their reaction. She was certain her reaction would make better TV.

So, after admiring herself for a moment, Veronika put both hands to her face and mouthed a shocked O, just like they did in the show. Then she raised her eye-brows and extended a few of her fingers to frame her mouth as she'd seen participants do.

Yes.

She would make far better TV viewing, particularly in a show where looking awesome was a requirement.

—

Libby tapped the wall so Wulfie would find his way to the pipe leading up from the hall. Then she ran ahead, past her parents' room and Rex's. She couldn't tap the walls anywhere she was likely to be seen, so she thought she'd wait in the spare room directly above Rex's room. She could tap that wall wall loudly enough for Wulfie to hear it down the pipe and know which way to go.

—

By then, Wulfie had reached the steep pipe that ran alongside Libby's parents' room. Since humming had made him sleepy, he was doing his times tables to stay awake. As Veronika sat back down on her bed, feeling wonderfully self-satisfied, he began to climb. Veronika put on her headphones, inadvertently changing the dial to the highest Hear Flies Breathe setting, and unpaused the show.

When the show began it was all creepy music and tiptoeing into a basement, so it came as quite a surprise when Veronika heard the wall behind her say – quite clearly – 'Nine threes are twenty-six.'

Without thinking, she answered, 'Twenty-seven.'

Before Wulfie could say – also without thinking – 'Thank you', Veronika sat up with a jolt, bumping the headboard against the wall. The *thonk*, landing right beside his head, surprised Wulfie, who lost his grip. He slid all the way down to the bottom of the pipe and, thanks to her headphones, Veronika heard everything: his claws scraping the pipe, the hurried breathing, the occasional *ouch* ...

Libby's stepmother knew all the signs of ghostly infestation, thanks to her favourite show. The air going suddenly cold. A strange smell that comes from nowhere and lingers. A movement out of the corner of your eye. Even, if you were lucky, someone walking towards the bed, looking entirely real but then suddenly disappear-ing.

Ghosts did *not* do sums.

She had taken off her headphones and was trying to decide whether she had heard anything at all when Rex ran in. He was shouting about Libby being mad and the sink growling at him. 'Hey, you're watching that ghost-hunting show! Do they, like, blast the ghosts into bits of goo and squelchy stuff?'

'I'm watching the programme to think of things to scare people like your sister with ...' said Veronika and threw him a bar of chocolate from her private stash so that he would go away.

—

With no sign of Wulfie getting closer, Libby ran downstairs, tapping and listening at walls to try and work out how far he'd got. She narrowly missed being seen by Rex, who was charging into his room clutching a chocolate bar as she slipped down to the hall to begin tapping the walls from the beginning again.

—

Wulfie was concentrating so hard on climbing silently, while also listening carefully so he wouldn't get surprised again, that he missed the right turn into the pipe that crossed Libby's parents' ceiling. As Veronika stepped into the shower, pre-lathered with lavender shower gel, the wulfen was climbing past Rex's room instead.

Libby's stepmother had decided that her brain was strained from overwork. She would focus on the future and visualise how perfect her new home would be. Impatient, she turned the shower on and off and on.

And off and on.

The water dribbled out, since it had to squeeze past a small purple wulfen who was creating a blockage in the water pipe.

Frustrated, Veronika turned it off. *The sooner we are in a new house with a wet room just for me, the better*, she thought. Because it would be *hers*, the new house. With underfloor heating, square rooms and all new furniture.

She sighed contentedly and tried the shower once more.

—

Wulfie was in trouble again. He was getting wet and the water above his head was getting heavier until the wulfen was swept down the pipes towards the shower, where he hit his head and blocked the flow completely.

'Ouch,' he said.

Veronika turned the water off and listened.

This gave Wulfie time to wriggle backwards, pushing through the water. He'd just reached the supply pipe, when Veronika walloped the shower unit and slipped, landing on her bum as the shower suddenly came on full blast.

—

Hearing the shower, Libby panicked. Wulfie couldn't get swept away again! She ran through the house, the watch-that-wasn't now ticking away in her hand. She tapped on the walls, tracing him up and round rooms. Wulfie had already been exhausted – Libby didn't think he'd have the strength to fight his way back up from the main again.

Fortunately, being the higgledy-piggledy house that it was, the pipes in Libby's home rarely went right and left. They went up and over and under and around and, as Veronika showered, Wulfie was *thunk*ed and *thomp*ed and *whomp*ed around the building.

It was like the worst and wettest rollercoaster ever.

—

After her shower, as the water still ran through the pipes, Veronika could hear *thunk*ing and *whunk*ing and the occasional *ouch* from inside the walls. She got dressed and decided to go downstairs to rest on the sofa in the sitting room.

There, she tucked into an extra-large bar of dark chocolate and shouted for Libby to fetch her a cup of tea.

Libby's dad remembered that he'd forgotten to brush his teeth and headed upstairs, passing Libby on the way as she dashed around following the pipe noises. 'I see you've got that watch working again,' he said as he pottered into the bathroom, but Libby was already on the floor below.

He was humming a tune from a musical about inventors that he thought he might write some day. It would definitely have dragons in it.

And maybe a unicorn.

—

As Veronika was shouting for a cup of tea for the third time, a painting on the wall of the sitting room suddenly shifted sideways. Pictures moving – now that was definitely a sign of the paranormal! When the picture began to spin, Veronika gasped. *Could it be ...?*

Behind the wall, a tiny wulfen was running on the nail from which the painting hung, as if it were a very tiny treadmill. The hole made by the nail got bigger and bigger. And, yes, there shouldn't have been a nail piercing a water pipe but Veronika had hung this particular picture in this particular place herself because it was a portrait of her looking magnificent. Up until now, the nail had held, meaning there had never been even the tiniest leak.

Veronika approached the wall as Wulfie lost his footing and fell.

He only fell a little bit because his tail snagged on the very same nail. Which is why Veronika very clearly heard the wall say, 'Owwwww,' because it isn't nice to be snagged.

Wulfie pulled himself up to perch back on the nail. He shook one leg dry at a time and decided to wait for Libby to find him again. Each time he shook a paw, Veronika's picture shuddered, and he had just got himself dry when minty toothpaste-flavoured water came down the pipe.

It wasn't a lot, but Wulfie liked mint. Wulfen pups are kept in beds of mint until they are able to walk – it stops other animals from attacking them – and so mint made him feel happy, like a sort of happiness *fuel*. He opened his mouth for a taste as it passed.

While keeping his eyes tightly closed.

—

The watch-that-wasn't ticked louder as Libby reached the hall. It was leading her to the sitting room, but Veronika was in there, so Libby waited behind the door of Dad's Inventing Room, trying to work out what she could do to make Veronika leave.

—

Inside the sitting room, Veronika's brain was ticking over, step by step: footsteps, breathing and ouching were one thing, but a spinning picture was quite another! She tapped the wall with a shiny knuckle.

And the wall tapped back, thinking she was Libby.

Veronika jumped. Her heart was in her mouth. She smiled with excitement. *What to ask?* It was as if she was nine years old again, only instead of Ilda talking to the ghost in their grandparents' house, it was her.

She tapped the wall again, firmly.

'Is that you?' said Wulfie, hopefully.

'It is I, Veronika!' She spoke in a voice she thought sounded impressive. 'Do I know you?'

Wulfie didn't answer. He wasn't meant to talk to Veronika or Rex or anyone apart from Libby and Nazim.

'Tap once for yes and twice for no.'

Wulfie tapped once. He was feeling lonely and didn't think tapping would hurt.

'Are you on the other side ...?' asked Veronika.

Libby's stepmother was asking if he had crossed from the land of the living into the world of the dead but Wulfie, thinking she meant was he on the other side of the wall, tapped back. Because he was.

Veronika had to prevent herself from skipping on the spot. She could hardly believe her luck – but she tried to remain calm to get all the information she could. 'Did you live in this house?'

Tap.

'Do you know who I am?'

Tap.

'Are you a ghost?'

'That's funny,' said Rex, coming into the room. 'Now you're talking to yourself too.'

'*Ssh,*' said Veronika sharply, as Wulfie thought back to Libby's definition. A ghost was someone who missed the people it loved.

'I think so,' he said, since he wasn't sure if one tap or two was correct.

Veronika punched the air. 'Don't move,' she said to the wall, pushing Rex out of the room ahead of her. 'I'll be right back.'

As soon as they left the room, Libby slipped in.

Chapter 10

Before Libby could work out which wall Wulfie was stuck behind, Veronika returned with Libby's dad, who was saying, 'Are you sure? The pipes do tend to rattle and wail,' and with Rex, looking smug.

'Of course I'm sure!' Veronika was not happy to see Libby in the room. 'What are you doing in here?'

'I was looking for you,' said Libby quickly, 'to see if you'd like a cup of tea.'

Veronika handed Rex her phone, instructing him to 'Film everything' before crossing over to the wall where her portrait hung. She had decided to try out the lines she'd heard on her favourite TV show, and spoke in single syllables, as if a ghost must be hard of hearing, being dead. 'Are – you – a – live?'

Well, Wulfie thought, *I'm a wulfen, not a 'live', whatever that is,* so he tapped twice for no and Veronika positively beamed. Libby's heart went out to her wulfen friend. He needed to be saved, not turned into an exhibit for her stepmother to play ghost hunter with, but there was nothing she could do.

'Are you trapped between our world and yours?' asked Veronika in an echoey voice. She felt like she was on TV already.

Behind the wall Wulfie decided that, well, he wasn't in Lupuslandia and he wasn't in Libby's world, not properly. So he tapped once for 'yes'.

'What – do – you – want?'

Wulfie took a deep breath. Remembering what Libby had said about ghosts, he decided that it might be safe to talk so long as Veronika didn't know he was Wulfie. 'I'm lost,' he said. 'And I'm tired of being wet.'

'What is your name?' said Veronika.

Wulfie didn't answer since he couldn't say Wolfgang Amadeus Rachmaninoff the Third or Wulfie. Veronika only knew him as a dog and dogs didn't talk, or have middle names, or get small enough to be wherever he was.

Impatient, Veronika thumped the wall to his right, making him jump. The nail that had been holding the painting bounced out and her portrait crashed to the ground, narrowly missing two of her toes. Wulfie fell down to the bottom of the pipe, landing in the bend where it turned to go under Dad's Inventing Room.

He moaned, feeling sorry and sore.

The moan curled up through the pipes and made Veronika shudder. She didn't notice the tiniest droplet of water oozing out from where the nail had been.

'Do you smell that?' she said, beaming and sniffing the air. 'Lavender and mint! Ghosts leave signature smells.' Veronika moved towards Dad on the far side of the room. 'What's the name of that stinky old mariner, your great-grandfather?' she said.

'Zebediah wasn't stinky!' said Libby.

'Zebediah!' said Veronika. 'That's who it is!' When nobody responded, she carried on. 'The ghost said he was wet! Probably drowned, the stupid man. What more proof do you need?'

Already, she could see herself talking to the camera, being interviewed by the ghost-hunter series presenters. How beautiful she would look on TV! 'I have a very important call to make,' she said, heading out of the room.

Rex trotted after her, like a lapdog hoping for a treat, and Dad retreated to his Inventing Room next door. As quickly as she could, Libby leaned in towards the wall. 'Wulfie, it's me. You're not lost,' she said. 'You're just a bit mislaid.'

'I'm so tired,' said her wulfen friend quietly.

Libby felt the watch-that-wasn't ticking in her pocket. 'I know,' she said. 'And the roof is too far away. For now, you need to get to one of the dry pipes and rest up. There's one that has a sort of shelf in it and you can stay there until it's safe to move—'

'Telling the ghost that you're an idiot or just stupid and nobody likes you?' Rex stomped back in. 'Mum says I'm to stay here filming the wall in case something else happens.' He kicked the skirting.

'Stop it!' Libby stepped in front of him.

But Rex was bored. He thumped the wall. 'Hey, Ghostie, what tricks can you do?'

Wulfie stayed quiet. He knew that was what Libby needed him to do right now, but when nothing happened, Rex pinched Libby's arm. 'Tell him to do some tricks.'

'Ouch,' she said, moving away. 'Why should he perform for you?'

Inside the pipe, Wulfie began to grow. He couldn't help it. He hated hearing Rex being mean to his best friend.

'Go on, Libby,' said Rex. 'Make the ghost do something!'

A bulge appeared in the wall behind Rex as he said, 'Tell him to make things fly about and hit your head.'

'Don't listen,' Libby shouted to Wulfie desperately. 'Please ignore him!'

The bulge nudged Rex's elbow. As he turned, what seemed like the imprint of a hand with claws appeared in the wall, reaching for his head. Rex's mouth opened like a goldfish expecting food to appear. There was a moment when it looked as if he might crumple up on the floor like a used sweet wrapper but, instead, he fled.

—

Downstairs, Veronika put down the phone and poured herself a glass of water. Feeling very proud of herself, she took a deep drink that tasted vaguely of socks and old cheese and spat it into the sink as Rex ran in. 'A hand ... A claw ... The wall!'

Slightly jealous of her son, who seemed to have made the ghost reveal himself, Veronika checked that Rex had filmed 'the Bulge' before sending him up to his room to recover.

Then she went to see the wall for herself.

—

'Can you remember the directions?' said Libby through the wall.

'Yes,' said Wulfie, hoping he could.

'Okay. I love you, Wulfie, but go now!' Libby whispered as she heard her stepmother's footsteps approaching. 'I'll come and find you as soon as I can.'

'The water tastes foul again,' Veronika shouted into Dad's room next door. 'Can you empty the tank immediately?'

Libby rushed out into the hall as Dad came out of the Inventing Room. 'We shouldn't do anything that might disturb the ghost,' she said, thinking quickly. 'And water might. Because you think it's Zebediah, right? And he drowned.'

Veronika was frowning. The scary sort of frown that made you look away, but Libby held firm. 'Besides, strange smells ... Didn't you say they were a sign of a ghost?' she said.

Strange sounds came from above as Wulfie crawled along the pipe in the ceiling, singing a wulfen lullaby to himself to keep his spirits up.

'And strange noises,' said Libby. 'Perhaps if the water tastes funny, it means he's *in* the water?'

Chapter 11

Having pointed to the kitchen, Veronika waited until Libby and her dad sat down at the end of the kitchen table and she was certain that she had their full and undivided attention. 'I didn't want *Zebediah* to overhear but suffice to say—' She looked at Dad then Libby – briefly – before staring into the distance and saying, as dramatically as she could, '*Most Horribly Haunted House TV*!'

Nobody responded. Libby really wanted to check on Wulfie, and Dad was frowning in a way that said 'I have an invention that needs attention'.

Disappointed, Veronika held up her favourite magazine and read the ad aloud: '"Bumps in the night? Are teapots flying across the room, narrowly missing the mole at the end of your nose?"'

Dad finally said what Libby was thinking, 'What has that got to do with us?'

Veronika sighed. 'The new presenter is Jasper Juniper Moon,' she said. 'The one who did the TV show on which my sister Ilda behaved like a puppy. I sent them Rex's video footage ...' She paused, as though taking in the enormity of what she was about to say. 'They are coming to assess the house,' she said. 'For the current series.' Her chin lifted a little higher. 'In two hours' time.'

Libby wanted to say, *What's the point if you're selling the house?* but until Wulfie was safely home, she had to play along. Besides, when the TV people arrived, everyone would be so distracted, Wulfie could make a run for the vent pipe and it wouldn't even matter if he made a noise.

Veronika was busy giving instructions, like the captain of a cruise ship. 'We need this house to look haunted yet utterly filmable,' she said, turning to Libby's dad. 'Light bulbs – can you change them all to weaker, more flickery ones? And can you make the doors creak?'

She knew she had to phrase her orders as questions for her husband to hear. At least Libby was easier. 'I want cobwebs in the corners. Use your father's re-webber thingy. The rug in the hall looks far too new. Swap it with your stringy bedroom one. And open your skylight and door. Haunted houses always have draughty stairwells. Then you can go to the shop and buy some bottled water and biscuits for our visitors' tea.'

—

Utterly exhausted after struggling up the pipes, Wulfie lay down on the safe 'shelf' on the other side of Rex's bedroom wall. He was tired of being tired. Unfortunately for Rex, the 'shelf' lay directly behind his headboard, so when Rex muttered, 'Stupid Mum, stupid ghost, stupid Libby!' to himself, Wulfie heard every word.

Now, Wulfie *could* have kept quiet, but he was a wulfen. Rex was mean to Libby all the time and he'd never had the chance to *talk* to Rex before, since dogs don't talk ... Some opportunities are too good to waste. He shook himself awake and deepened his voice.

'Hello, Rex,' he began.

—

Rex tumbled down the stairs, pale as a ghost who has just seen a ghost. 'It's … The ghost is … It said …' He pointed up the stairs. 'In my …'

Veronika was peeved. The ghost had now spoken to her son as well as to her – which made it all a bit less special. But Libby relaxed for the first time all day. This 'haunting' of her step-brother meant Wulfie was safe.

For now.

Rex remembered the worst bit: 'IT KNEW MY NAME!'

Looking at Rex's face, Veronika remembered that

children being scared made for good TV. She slipped an arm around her son's shoulders and chucked him under the chin. 'That's my boy.' She dispatched Dad and Libby to their chores and took Rex to the kitchen for a cup of hot chocolate.

Now she knew Rex's room was free, Libby rolled up the hall rug and headed upstairs. Leaving the rug on the landing, Libby tiptoed into Rex's room and rested her hand on the wall, near where she believed Wulfie to be. 'Are you okay?'

'I am now,' said Wulfie. He'd used his last ounce of oomph scaring Rex, but the sound of Libby's voice made him feel safe.

'There will be TV people coming in two hours,' said Libby. 'Try to sleep till then and get your strength back because when they arrive you'll have to go back into the pipes—'

'I don't want to get wet again,' said Wulfie.

Libby wished she could smash the wall down and pluck him out. 'Oh, Wulfie, if there was another way … But I promise you there won't be any more water, and the vent pipe is the only way I know for you to get home.'

Wulfie mustered all his wulfen-ness and fighting spirit. 'Okay,' he said. 'I can do it.'

'I know you can,' said Libby. 'You're the bravest wulfen I know.'

'I'm the *only* wulfen you know!'

'And I know how brave you can be. Right, this is what you have to do ...'

Chapter 12

A yellow convertible with red leather seats and go-faster stripes of fire pulled up outside number 1 Longish Strand Road as Libby fished out the enormous spool of silk ribbon from Zebediah's trunk. She put it in her knapsack, balanced her chair on her bed and placed her largest schoolbooks on top. Taking a very deep breath and feeling not a little bit scared, Libby climbed up.

She had barely hauled herself out through the skylight when the chair capsized and Rex kicked her bedroom door open. He liked kicking doors open – and shut – often for no reason at all. It was a pity, he thought, that Libby's door didn't have glass in it. He bet he could have kicked the door open hard enough to smash it. 'Mum wants you to—'

Rex stopped, disappointed to find the room empty. He flexed his shoulders in a way he hoped would look as if he hadn't been recently scared twice by a stupid ghost. Up on the roof, Libby tied one end of the silk ribbon around the shaft of the pipe and the other around one of Dad's biscuits. As her step-brother stalked around her room below, she fed the biscuit down the ventilation pipe.

Rex knocked her chair and books off the bed, but that wasn't enough. He was looking for something mean to do to make up for Libby not being there to bully in person.

—

JJ Moon's lanky assistant, Peta, unpeeled herself from the cramped passenger seat of the convertible and wondered if she'd ever be able to stand up straight again.

She joined the presenter, who was looking beadily up at the house.

Number 1 Longish Strand Road hadn't been easy to find. As the first house to be built on the road, it was irrationally tucked into a newer terrace between numbers 12 (Mr H) and 13. Wider and taller than its neighbours, it had two extra floors that stuck slightly forward, like the prow of a ship. It would definitely look good on TV.

JJ Moon liked to dress to match his role on whatever show he was presenting. It was like a disguise that allowed him to hide his shyness and project confidence on TV. So today he was dressed as his idea of a paranormal investigator, in a cloak with a collar and a red bowtie. His trousers had pineapple-coloured stripes and made him look tall, although he still barely came up to Peta's shoulders.

So far, the houses they'd seen for the new series had been disappointing. There hadn't been a single polter-geist tossing things around or a shimmer of a ghostly apparition. They hadn't even filmed spaghetti dancing on a countertop. He hoped the footage they'd been sent of number 1 Longish Strand Road was the real thing.

He'd hate to have worn his lucky trousers for nothing.

—

Upstairs in Libby's room, Rex discovered that the ship painting propped on her desk was handily close to some marker pens. Horrified, Libby watched from the roof as he added a plank, a pirate's flag and some dead bodies hanging off the ship's sails. Then he drew some luminous yellow sharks in the water and a spare leg with blood spewing from it.

And there was nothing she could do.

—

Since the skylight and Libby's bedroom door were both open, the wind did exactly what Veronica wanted. It circled the chimney stack to gather speed, swooped past Libby and down into her room, then out past Rex, down the stairwell and into the hall. It gave the house a distinctly haunted feel, Veronika thought, as she opened the front door – now creaking nicely, thanks to Dad – to JJ Moon.

The presenter, however, was staring out at the street so that he could twirl when the door was answered. He liked the *floosh*ing sound his cloak made as it turned and settled. 'Jasper Juniper Moon,' he said, holding out a hand. 'Television presenter and, currently, paranormal investigator. And this is my assistant, Peta Maguire.'

—

Hearing his mother call him, Rex threw the ship picture on to Libby's bed and left the attic room. Only when she was certain he was gone did Libby lower herself down from the skylight. She dropped and tumbled onto the bed, like a parachute jumper landing on an airfield.

Having put the picture back on the desk – 'I'll fix you later, somehow,' she promised – Libby made a snuggery of clothes on the bed and topped it with her mother's blue jumper.

Now Wulfie would be able to land softly when he made it home.

Chapter 13

Peta rigged up a camera on a tripod in the sitting room, before loping off downstairs and into the back garden. While JJ Moon gathered all the background info about the house on camera, she would follow her hunches, sniffing out indications of ghostly infestation.

The garden was a mess of plaster and mud, but what was interesting was the woodwork Veronika had exposed on the back wall with the Master Blaster. It was as if the stern of a wooden ship had been incorporated into the brickwork. Peta took a photo on her phone. If there was a sea captain haunting the house, this would make a good backdrop for one of the interviews. She made her way inside and down to the cellar.

By the time Peta emerged into the kitchen, with cobwebs on her beanie, Libby was making up a tray for Veronika and JJ Moon. 'Will that tell you if there's a ghost in the house?' asked Libby, pointing at the device in Peta's hand. It looked like a television zapper, but it was one of the investigator's favourite devices.

'This,' said Peta, 'is a digital thermometer capable of measuring sudden drops in temperature.' She looked at Libby with what she thought was a wise and deeply psychic gaze, then circled the room, holding the device in front of her. 'A pocket of cold air could indicate the presence of a ghost.'

Finding nothing except a couple of biscuits, Peta frowned and headed upstairs without another word.

—

JJ Moon was in the front room, standing opposite Veronika, who was posed with one hand resting gently on 'the Wall'. 'When you're ready,' he said.

Veronika sighed in a way she felt was particularly filmic. 'Zebediah F Flanagan was born here in 1845, in this very room.' Veronika thought the addition of the room as his birthplace added extra oomph to her ghostly claims. 'Of course, he wasn't my ancestor. I come from landed aristocracy, though I don't happen to have proof of that, except in the shape of my nose.'

JJ Moon walked over to touch the slight indentation that remained in the wall and tried a tap or two, just in case. 'What makes you think it's him?' he said. 'And why would he choose to haunt you now?'

'Oh, I've always felt an affinity for old Zebbie. Ever since I married the love of my life—' Veronica pulled Libby's dad into shot. He blinked rapidly. 'Zebediah has become my ancestor too, hasn't he, darling?'

'I'm not sure that's entirely how it works,' said Dad.

Tightening her grip on his arm, Veronica dug a solitary heel into his toe. Dad stopped talking and moved away, glad he was wearing his steel-capped boots. Veronika smiled at JJ Moon in a way she thought would light up the small screen. 'They say he disappeared at sea, but is there any proof that he ever left this house?'

Before she could answer herself with a theatrical and resounding 'No!', Dad responded from the safety of his armchair: 'I suspect we'd have smelt him around. You see, Mr Moon, according to family legend, his daughter, my grandmother, had a very keen sense of smell, while dear Zebediah wasn't keen on bathing.' Dad was enjoying himself. 'He preferred to jump fully clothed into a lagoon whenever he met one. Trouble was, you have to be on a boat, mostly, to meet a lagoon so, in-between, he could – apparently – get quite whiffy.'

'He may be trapped in these walls still,' said Veronika, interrupting and gesturing at the patch of damp that was now visible where her painting had hung. 'This damp spot appeared on the wall right after he spoke to me, accompanied by the aroma of lavender and mint. Maybe it's a sea captain's version of ghost goo – I mean, ectoplasm,' she said.

She would insist they edited Dad's comments out of the final show.

—

As Libby took the tray of tea and biscuits upstairs, Peta emerged from Dad's Inventing Room. She pocketed another biscuit and carried on up the stairs without a word.

Back in the sitting room, JJ Moon was far more talkative. 'I've always wanted to see a ghost – that's why I was so delighted to be asked to present this show,' he said, as Libby poured his tea. He lined a handful of biscuits up along his left leg.

'Oh, me too!' said Veronika.

'Ah, but *you* have spoken with one,' he said.

Veronika beamed. 'Yes,' she said. 'Yes, I have.'

'When I was four, I named our dog Ghost,' said JJ Moon. 'That's how desperate I was.'

'Oh, I lied,' said Veronika, taking her cup from Libby. 'I convinced everyone at school that I'd seen a ghost in my grandmother's bathroom. I mean, why would a ghost be in a bathroom?'

'Perhaps the individual died in the shower,' said JJ Moon.

Veronika giggled. 'I didn't say it was a naked ghost!'

—

Wulfie was following Libby's instructions as quickly as he could when Veronika suggested she show JJ Moon the house's other 'haunted sites'. The instructions weren't easy. There were several 'second lefts' and 'down a bits' and 'up and round the rooms' before Wulfie found the biscuit at the end of the ribbon and began to pull himself up the long vent pipe.

All in all, his journey allowed for plenty of apparently ghostly *thonk*s and sounds of heavy breathing, seemingly within the very fabric of the house. Veronika smiled apologetically at the TV presenter, as if this was all entirely normal, and led him upstairs.

Wulfie's nose finally quivered out from the ventilation pipe onto the roof. After one deep, satisfying sniff, and before he pulled himself clear, the wulfen sighed the longest, happiest sigh – which echoed down through the pipes.

As if the house were a living, breathing thing.

Oblivious to the excitement within the house at this supposed proof of ghostly infestation, Wulfie took a couple more deep breaths before somersaulting through the skylight and landing with a satisfying *plop* into the nest of clothes on Libby's bed.

They folded around him like a cocoon.

—

Hearing the sigh through the pipes, Libby left the washing up and rushed upstairs, only slowing down to pass Peta, so as not to attract attention. The investigator was standing in the shower cubicle, eyes closed and listening hard – while in Rex's room opposite, JJ Moon was hearing how the ghost had threatened Rex through his wall.

Closing her bedroom door quietly behind her, Libby tiptoed over and lifted Wulfie ever so softly out of his nest. He was still tiny and fitted into her hand like a small ball of sodden fur. He licked her nose by way of a kiss. 'Oh, Wulfie,' she said, sitting down on the bed. 'I missed you so much.'

'I was so lost and so scared ...' He tried to shake himself properly dry, but being very, very tired all of a sudden, he fell asleep only half-shaken, still as small as a Siberian hamster. Libby dried his fur with her sleeves.

'There there,' she crooned. 'You're safe now.' The watch-that-wasn't-only-a-watch had almost stopped. She tucked it in beside him, the slow ticking like a heartbeat to soothe him.

—

Peta was on the
final flight of
stairs when her thermom-
eter indicated a cold spot
up ahead. Heart beating
happily, she opened Libby's door slowly
and quietly – so as not to disturb a ghost
– giving Libby just enough time to place Wulfie into
her pocket.

'Oh,' said the investigator, looking very disappointed. 'It's you.' She spun the thermometer around,
but it seemed confused.

Libby stroked Wulfie's head secretly, willing the investigator to leave so she could be alone with her friend, but Peta was now taking photos with her phone of the paintings leaning against the wall. 'Which one's Zebediah?' she asked.

'He's not there,' said Libby, trying not to giggle as Wulfie started snoring in her pocket and the vibrations tickled her hand.

The investigator was suddenly alert, staring around the room and waving her device about. 'That vibration,' she said. 'Do you hear it?'

Libby wrapped her hand around Wulfie's snout to muffle the sound and shook her head.

Why should she help Veronika now if proving the house was haunted would help her sell the house?

Chapter 14

Standing by the front door, JJ Moon accepted his cloak from Libby. 'The footage is compelling,' he said. 'The sounds we've heard today, coupled with the history of the house ...'

Veronika was holding her breath, waiting for the verdict. She had gone a shade of pink that was competing with her cerise suit.

'Normally we'd do a little more research,' said the presenter, straightening his bow-tie, 'but my colleague says she may have picked up vibrations and a pocket of cold air so ...'

Veronika gripped Rex by the hand. He tried to wriggle free and failed.

'It would have to be this weekend,' he said. 'Which means tomorrow afternoon onwards – and we would need to stay two nights.'

Veronika exhaled. 'Absolutely. Whatever you need.' She was using her smoothest, happiest voice, but Libby thought it still sounded as if it could slice carrots.

—

'No way am I having that trunk in my room!'

For years, Rex had made up truly scary stories for Libby, all involving Zebediah's trunk. Now, faced with having it in his room, he was far from happy. Veronika was not giving in. 'TV is a visual medium. If you are to be convincingly haunted on TV, there has to be something substantial belonging to Zebediah in your room – and this is it.' She gave the trunk a kick. 'See? Harmless.'

Dad suggested the trunk could be stood on one end, since Rex had so much *stuff*, but that was abandoned when Libby said that would make it look like a coffin. Instead, Rex's guitar was to be put down in Dad's Inventing Room, tons of clothes were picked up off the floor and stuffed into Libby's hands for the washing machine, while boxes of half-finished robots and half-played games were shoved under the bed and into the attic storage space beside Libby's room.

'You could always sleep in the trunk,' said Dad, 'to really connect.'

Libby was sure Dad was making fun of them because he winked at her before he headed downstairs with the guitar – but Veronika, being Veronika, paused, as if giving it serious thought.

'No!' said Rex, before she could agree. 'No way am I sleeping in it!'

'Of course not, darling,' said Veronika, with a hint of regret.

—

Rex's training began at bedtime, when Veronika made him watch several episodes of *Most Horribly Haunted House* with her. Then she began rehearsing his story for the show. 'This is what happened, darling boy,' she said. 'You woke up and saw Zebediah standing there. By the trunk.'

Rex looked uncomfortable.

'Remember,' his mother said, 'you are a student at Ms Emily's Academy of Drama and Dance and Doing Good Things. Now is your chance to shine.' She took a deep breath and continued. 'Zebediah looked you in the eye, and suddenly you felt everything he had ever felt. The cold water closing over you. The dark. The terrible thirst.'

Libby wasn't sure if being loved by Veronika was a healthy thing for any child.

'The seaweed tendrils wrapping round your feet ...' continued Veronika, fastening a cone collar around Rex's neck to make sure he slept badly and looked haunted when the TV crew returned the following day. 'I want you thinking of this all through the night, so it feels utterly real when you speak of it tomorrow.'

Veronika is even better at making up scary stories than Rex, thought Libby. But something in Libby that loved fairness sprang to the surface and, before she could think of how mean Rex had been to her over and over, she said, 'Zebediah didn't drown.'

Veronika swivelled round, her eyes as cold as a shark's – one that hasn't eaten for months.

'I'm just saying.' Libby tried to hold her ground. 'We don't know that Zebediah drowned. Dad says he might have gone off and married someone else, since his own wife had died. And even though he had loved her enormously, she did find his long beard a pain. I mean, she probably did. So he might have found someone who loved beards. Maybe.'

Veronika stood up and walked towards the door. 'Your point being?'

Forced backwards by her stepmother's advance, Libby couldn't stop the story she was creating. 'That he might have died of old age, on a rocking horse – or even a real horse, a white one – happy as anything.'

Veronika slammed the door shut in her step-daughter's face, but not before Libby saw what looked like a glimmer of thanks in Rex's eyes. He'd have forgotten by the time she saw him again, but it was nice to know there was a chance that her step-brother was human.

—

All evening, Wulfie slept in Libby's pocket, small as a glove. She took him out when she was changing for bed and then, with a couple of leg kicks and a great big yawn, he finally woke up and grew slowly back to his normal medium-puppy size. Libby had been gathering a pile of scraps in her other pockets all day, which was lucky because Wulfie was seriously hungry now.

'You were like a tiny hibernating bear,' she said. 'No, more like a purple hedgehog, if a hedgehog had fur.'

Full at last, Wulfie rolled onto his back beside her on the bed, almost purring with happiness.

Libby smiled and filled him in on all that had happened, but her wulfen friend was fast asleep again before she'd got through half of it and Libby wasn't far behind. It had been a long, long day.

—

It felt like Libby had only been asleep for moments when Veronika woke her at dawn with a list of instructions and chores for the day. Mist was coming in through the open skylight. Grateful for the warmth of the new hall rug under her feet, Libby still missed her threadbare one. She'd imagined whole worlds in its faded patterns.

'Do you have to go?' said Wulfie.

'I'll be back as soon as I can and you need to rest. Veronika's pretty serious about this ghost thing, so you need to stay out of sight.'

Wulfie shivered. 'I forgot about the ghost. Is it scary?'

'Oh, silly,' said Libby, hugging the wriggly purple bundle. 'The ghost was *you*!'

And then, seeing as Wulfie was still shivering and knowing how horrible it was to be alone and scared, she let him slip into her pocket – 'but no talking, or growing, or tying shoe-laces together when no-one's looking.'

Chapter 15

The mist was visible through all the windows as Libby headed downstairs, as if they were inside a cloud or on a foamy, ghostly sea. She wondered if the new owners of this house would ever realise how magical it was. She sighed and put that thought aside. Wulfie was safe and that was what mattered most.

Oddly enough, today's chores involved undoing most of Libby's normal chores. There was un-polishing and un-dusting and un-cobweb removal with Dad's re-webber. Then there was un-shaking of rugs and the hiding away of ornaments that looked new. After that, she had to tidy away all Veronika's clothes from the spare room – a room her stepmother regarded as a spare wardrobe – since this was to be *Most Horribly Haunted House*'s headquarters.

It was almost fun, thought Libby, as if she were eliminating all traces of her stepmother.

—

Rex looked haunted by the time he appeared for breakfast. He even forgot to drop crumbs from his toast for Libby to clean up. And he hadn't needed the cone collar to keep him awake, either. Veronika's stories and his experiences the day before, plus the trunk backlit by the moon, had been more than enough to make him sleepless.

He was an altogether nicer step-brother to have like this, thought Libby, when he was sleep-deprived.

Veronika, however, was definitely not.

She returned from the hairdresser's via a boutique, where she'd found a pale-green outfit she thought would make her glow on the night-vision cameras. She handed Libby a list of new instructions. 'I want to offer the TV crew three types of sandwiches,' she said. Reaching into her handbag, she pulled out a picture she'd ripped from a gossip magazine at the hairdresser's. 'Make them look like these.'

Rex was sitting on the sofa trying to sleep. Veronika poked him awake.

'And hang up some of those old pictures,' she said to Libby. 'The grisly ones – that one with the glassy eyes and the woman with scabby skin.'

The 'scabby' skin was the result of the oil paint cracking in sunlight, while Libby thought the glassy eyes looked wise and forgiving. She would be happy to put them up again.

Veronika wandered towards The Wall where the damp spot was growing. She traced the outline of it, trying to decide if it was the shape of a boat or a sea captain.

'One last thing,' said Veronika before she left the room. She handed Libby what looked like a really ugly coffee pot without a spout. 'Fill this thing with ashes from the fireplace. I'll get your father to remove the handle later.'

'What's it meant to be?' said Libby.

'A funeral urn, of course! Don't you know that every haunted house needs an urn?'

'They can't be Zebediah's ashes,' said Dad, reasonably, from behind his journal, 'since we don't know where or how he died.'

'So think up someone, then. A grisly old aunt who was known for killing off her husbands. Or maybe they could be your first wife's ashes?'

Everyone in the room went still. Even Rex knew this wasn't something you said in front of the daughter of that first wife, that daughter being Libby.

'They couldn't be her ashes,' said Dad, putting his arm around Libby and giving her a squeeze.

'My mum is only mislaid,' said Libby. 'She's a famous explorer and you don't have an urn of ashes when you've been mislaid.'

'Of course not,' said Veronika quickly. 'I was speaking imaginatively!'

It was too much for Libby. Dad's arm was still nearby, so she risked responding: 'What's the point of doing this show if you're going to sell the house anyway?'

Veronika turned sharply and caught Libby with a very direct, very icy stare. Her eyes were like headlamps, thought Libby, wincing; the sort of headlamps that generally mean you can expect to be run over imminently. 'If this house were famous,' said Veronika, forcing herself to smile at her step-daughter, 'for example, the most haunted house in the whole of Dublin ... Ireland, even ... Why, I wouldn't *dream* of selling it.'

Libby frowned. Veronika did love all things famous. Look at how she'd fawned over the TV producer. Her sister Ilda had been the same. She'd been willing to lie and mistreat dogs just to be famous.

—

Wulfie woke from a little doze and smelt something so beautifully icky that he found himself climbing quietly out of Libby's pocket and following the smell into Veronika's handbag, where he began guzzling a leaky tube of face cream. One of its ingredients was urea, which was pretty close to urine, so it tasted delightfully disgusting.

And since disgusting things make wulfens smell sweet, the most beautiful aroma swept up from Veronika's handbag towards her nose and made her feel suddenly kindly towards those around her. Nice smells often do that, but nice smells from a wulfen are especially powerful – which is handy when the person is as nasty and mean as Veronika.

The change was almost instantaneous. Veronika lifted Libby's chin with a handful of long fingernails on which she had painted skulls and crossbones. Her voice was soft as butter. 'Oh, don't look so sad, darling,' she said. 'I am going to be on TV and I *will* be amazing ... You can be on TV with me and be amazing too ...'

Libby sniffed the air. That sweet smell ... Wulfie! She checked her pocket with her hand. Empty. She looked around frantically.

Veronika was caressing Dad's moustache as if it were a stray ferret that had somehow landed on his face and settled down for a long, soft sleep. And she didn't like anything with legs and fur! Libby spotted the tip of Wulfie's tail peeping out of Veronika's handbag as her stepmother fluffed up Dad's hair, adding inches to his height.

Now, as far as her family was concerned, Wulfie was meant to be a dog – but not the sort of dog that fitted into a bag and *especially* not Veronika's handbag.

'Shouldn't you be trying on your new outfit?' said Libby, spinning her stepmother towards the door while scooping Wulfie quickly out of the handbag and hiding him behind her back.

'What a lovely idea,' said Veronika, stroking Libby on the head as if she were a small child she actually liked.

—

By the time Libby had made sandwiches for the *Most Horribly Haunted House* team, Veronika had entirely recovered from her spell of being nice, though she was still feeling rather confused. She called for an avocado and some cucumber. There was time for one last facial before the filming began.

'When the team arrives later this afternoon, apart from fetching and carrying, I want you and that dog of yours to stay out of the way,' she said. 'Nobody wants a scruffy child and their mangy dog on TV. And we do want the house to do well on screen, don't we?'

Libby nodded.

'Good. Now, bring some coffee to my room in half an hour. I must be full of vim for the cameras!'

Chapter 16

'The house has to be haunted, but how?' Libby paced her room and Wulfie paced beside her, flicking his tail from side to side in a way that helped him think.

'I can talk behind their backs and then be acting like a dog when they turn around?' said Wulfie.

Libby shook her head. 'Too risky.'

'Or I could be a really big shadow but shrink to mouse size or sneeze them frozen so I can escape unseen?'

'I'm sorry, Wulfie. They'll have cameras all over the place.'

Wulfie sat down on the rug. 'I don't want to go back into the pipes,' he said.

Libby stopped and picked him up for a cuddle. 'You're not going back into them. You hear me? You are never,

ever going back into those pipes.' She buried her face in his fur until it made her sneeze. 'Maybe they'll have enough with what Rex and Veronika say about the ghost in their interviews.'

—

The *Most Horribly Haunted House* van pulled up outside early that afternoon. Veronika greeted them, by now so full of coffee that if she turned around too suddenly she'd start spinning and disappear into a hole drilled into the floor by her heels. She'd been banging walls for the past half-hour, warning her 'Ghostie' to be properly scary 'or else!'

Libby felt pretty sure this was not the sort of thing you should say to a ghost.

Unless you wanted to make it mad.

Peta set to work immediately. Soon extension leads were wriggling around banisters and draped over doors, as cameras were installed facing the 'hot spots'. With Wulfie in her pocket – so he'd see how dangerous it was for him to get up to anything wulfen while the film crew was there – Libby followed Peta around, holding flexes and untangling leads for her.

There was even going to be a camera facing the trunk in Rex's room: the trunk over which her step-brother had already tripped five times. He had bumps on his knees to prove it. If Libby had believed in ghosts, she'd have said her great-great-grandfather had a sense of humour.

Dad wandered into the spare room, attracted by all the gadgets on display. Peta was only too glad to show off to an interested audience. 'I've rigged it so all data feeds back here,' she said, tapping her laptop. 'Any change at all, any sound or variation in temperature or movement on any of the cameras, and I get pinged on my headphones!'

'Is that a thermal-imaging camera?' said Dad. 'Picks up infra-red light, right?'

Peta nodded. She turned it to capture JJ Moon as he set up his chair in the corner – he looked red and yellow and vaguely human-shaped on its screen.

'How does that work?' said Libby.

'Blue means cold. If it's moving and it has a shape of some sort, then it could well be a ghost.'

'Why are ghosts always cold?' said Libby. Having slept two nights at the top of a wind tunnel, she thought being always cold couldn't be nice.

'I think the idea is they need our energy to appear, so they suck heat out of the atmosphere,' said Dad.

'Exactly,' said Peta, beaming at Dad, her teeth either very white or her lips very red.

'Wouldn't it be better if the camera was mounted on wheels?' said Dad. 'Rigged up to track cold spots automatically?'

'The motion might spook the spooks,' said Peta, feeling witty. 'Quite often there isn't a lot to see. That's when this little beauty comes into her own.' Peta held out her digital voice recorder. 'It's so sensitive that it records sounds human ears can't hear. Ultra-high frequency sounds.' She bit into a protein bar and, almost on cue, Wulfie's first two stomachs growled. (The third was still asleep after the trauma of swallowing so much water the day before.)

'Sshh,' said Peta. 'It's picking something up.'

She spun round with her camera, looking for a trace of blue. There was a vague *purple* aura near the girl – as if the blue was underneath the red – but that wasn't possible. The girl was totally real.

Libby pinched her pocket shut. But then, since she needed the house to be haunted, she shrugged. 'We hear vibrations and strange noises all the time. We hardly notice them any more.'

—

As soon as the team had eaten their fill of sandwiches and tea, work began, and Wulfie agreed to stay out of sight in Libby's room. Having turned off all the lights for atmosphere, Peta filmed JJ Moon's introduction on the stairs. 'Is this misshapen Victorian building haunted by the lonesome ghost of the man who made it his own?' he said, walking slowly down from the top of the house, watched by Libby's ancestors on the walls.

'This troubled sea captain, whose beard was said to be so long it touched the ground, could he be reliving his death? The smell of seaweed would seem to suggest so ...'

After this, JJ Moon interviewed Veronika outside the bathroom, in front of the two paintings she liked least. She told her version of the story about who Zebediah was and how desperate he had been to communicate with her – following her from room to room. Libby didn't mind *what* lies her stepmother told any more because now she needed the TV crew to believe the house really was haunted – *famously* haunted – because then Veronika wouldn't sell the house and Libby would never have to move.

While they waited for it to get darker outside, JJ Moon filmed Peta in the spare room, explaining about electro-magnetic rays and thermal pockets in a whisper for the audience, and then they stood mother and son in front of 'The Wall', with Veronika's own portrait along-

side. Veronika had dressed Rex in army khaki, with a cross around his neck.

Libby grinned. Veronika was getting her ghosts mixed up with her vampires.

As Veronika recounted all that had happened in the room up until she'd left Rex there – she didn't see the point of mentioning that Libby had been there too – Rex stood, frozen and unspeaking, in front of the camera.

After three takes, all Peta had managed to get out of him was a couple of 'I ...', two 'It was ...' and one 'Hand ...'

Libby hopped in. The house needed to be haunted, and fast, before they lost interest. 'Rex was so brave,' she said. 'When the hand came through the wall—'

'*Through* the wall?' said JJ Moon. 'I thought it was only an impression in the wall?'

'Oh no,' said Libby, keeping her fingers crossed behind her back. 'It was a hand. It was long and thin and almost bony.' Libby had been treated to Rex's scary bedtime stories for years and she'd learnt a thing or two. 'The sort you'd imagine reaching up out of a really, really old grave. Or from a shipwreck at the bottom of the ocean.'

Veronika butted in to explain that, since the damp spot had been under her portrait, it was 'very clear who he wanted to connect with here: Me and my son. The girl was entirely incidental.'

Chapter 17

Peta and JJ Moon spent the next few hours recording themselves asking questions in the 'haunted zones' with all the lights off, hoping their digital recorder might pick up an answer that the human ear couldn't hear.

While they worked, Veronika had Libby make more sandwiches for the team as she baked one of her spectacular cakes for the following day. She thought she might decorate it to look like Zebediah himself, but then decided he was too ugly. Since this cake would feature on TV, it had to be magnificent. *Spook-tacular!* she thought, settling on making it look like a haunted house.

When the investigators reached Libby's room, Wulfie shrank and hid behind the pictures. Peta's camera was showing something not quite blue *somewhere* in the room. 'I got a vibration here yesterday,' she said, waving her thermometer around until she settled on a painting of a woman in a mantilla, looking fierce. Something bluish – or maybe purple-ish – was showing up on the thermal camera, similar to the unusual colour she'd seen on screen for the first time the day before.

Behind the painting, Wulfie held his breath.

'Interesting,' Peta said.

And, for the camera, JJ Moon asked, 'Perhaps there are more than two ghosts haunting number 1 Longish Strand Road?'

Having delivered the food to the spare room where the crew were resting, Libby had to wait until the team moved back downstairs before she could crawl off to bed, exhausted, though not forgetting to bring some extra egg-and-onion sandwiches up for Wulfie.

'You were so good today, staying here quiet and safe,' she said and fell asleep snuggling him.

—

Wulfie woke in the middle of the night, ravenously hungry. The Spitglossums, who lived in his third stomach, had woken out of hibernation mode to find their larder – stomach number three – empty of food. They were kicking up a racket to let Wulfie know they needed feeding! It was like having a handful of very angry dinosaurs in his tummy.

Or one of his tummies.

Since he knew he couldn't leave the room, Wulfie jumped down off the bed and ate Libby's school uniform, which was waiting to go in the wash. Then he spat it out and licked it clean – because he also knew he shouldn't really eat her school uniform. Unfortunately, this only made his Spitglossums angrier, so he ate the contents of her bin – cardboard, pencil shavings, tissues, the lot; but even that wasn't enough because the Spitglossums had woken the Stinky Sigustingbugs in his throat and everyone else in-between.

Wulfie was full of wriggly things that wanted to be fed – RIGHT THIS MINUTE!

In desperation, he tried to wake Libby so she could fetch him some food, but she was deeply asleep, dreaming of finding the beautiful and terribly remote island on which her mother had been mislaid during her last exploration.

Wulfie made a decision.

If he kept small and moved quickly, he was sure he could avoid the cameras and get to the kitchen without anyone noticing. He'd find some of Libby's dad's stinky cheese – the Spitglossums liked that – but, just in case he got caught on camera, Wulfie pulled on the old hat with feathers as a disguise.

As Wulfie tiptoed downstairs, Peta was in the spare room, daydreaming about the future. Of the day when she would be so famous she'd be known as Peta the

Psychic, with her own TV show and her own agency, hired to travel the world and talk to ghosts.

The first time Wulfie had registered on Peta's thermal-imaging device, in Libby's pocket, he had shown up as not quite purple, but the trouble with an empty wulfen stomach is that it gets cold. Really cold. As if you're carrying a small freezer section around inside you. This meant that, as Wulfie crept past the spare room, his third stomach showed up on Peta's device as a sharp, shiny blue thermal form, both round and moving.

And therefore, most importantly for the psychic, as not necessarily human.

Peta quickly scanned the data coming into the laptop. Her digital recorder was catching what sounded like small banshees wailing. She couldn't know it, but this was the Spitglossums getting excited at the prospect of food.

If she had been a bloodhound, Peta's nose would have twitched, dropped to the floor and dragged her out onto the landing. As it was, she quietly unfolded herself from her chair – tricky when you have long legs – grabbed her camera in one hand and her thermometer in the other, and tracked the blue, fast-moving blur down the stairs, leaving JJ Moon fast asleep.

The temptation to catch a ghost all by herself was too strong.

—

Hearing footsteps behind him, Wulfie tiptoed into Rex's room on the floor below. Rex was in bed, snuggling the comfort 'blankie' he'd had as a baby. Shaped like a lion, with yellow teeth and a missing ear, it smelt of drool and dribbled food, of ear wax and nose wipings.

Wulfie lifted the lion reverentially, replacing it with the one-eyed rabbit from the old trunk before swallowing the blankie whole. Sadly, the Spitglossums weren't in the mood for 'slow food' like fabric. They wanted food that would speed past everyone else and come straight to stomach number three. Since Peta was breathing heavily outside Rex's door, Wulfie slipped out of the window and down the back wall.

It was only when a camera at the back door pinged on, catching a blur of something sliding in the kitchen window, that Peta moved.

The wulfen was devouring a chunk of smelly cheese under the kitchen table by the time she tiptoed in. 'Show yourself to me,' she whispered, as the sweetest smell curled out from under the table.

Was it honey and marshmallows or kisses and hugs? she wondered.

Before she could decide, Peta found herself lying down under the table, snuggling her camera and closing her eyes, feeling happy all over. She didn't wake up until several minutes after Wulfie had crept quietly past her and away.

Keeping himself small and fast, and clear of cameras, the wulfen sped back up to the top of the house, where he made himself tiny, slipped under Libby's bedroom door and crawled up onto her bed. His divine aroma wafted into Libby's dream-world reunion with her long-lost mother, and she smiled happily in her sleep.

Chapter 18

'Nothing human could have moved so fast – to go in one room and reappear three floors below!' Peta was uncomfortably aware that what she was describing sounded more like a vampire than a ghost. She helped herself to her tenth slice of toast as Libby refilled the teapot. 'Then there was this bewitching smell and I was instantly powerless.'

JJ Moon added a fifth spoonful of sugar to his tea and dipped a slice of toast in it so that half the marmalade slid off into the tea. 'You should have woken me,' he said with a frown.

—

Upstairs, Rex emerged from a very deep sleep to find his blankie transformed into a one-eyed stuffed rabbit. He threw it out of his room as hard as he could. It bounced down the stairs and landed in the hall with a thump.

Even JJ Moon jumped.

An unearthly shriek followed the rabbit down the stairs. Peta grabbed her camera and, quick as a blink, the paranormal investigators were out of the kitchen and flying upstairs. Libby followed slowly, her steps leaden on the stairs.

—

Veronika felt the shriek was particularly impressive. So did Mr H next door, who resisted the urge to hide under his bed when he heard it. As Dad arrived up from his Inventing Room, Veronika ushered Peta and JJ Moon into the bathroom and pointed at a perfectly harmless vanity cabinet. Rex stayed behind his mother, ready to scarper downstairs and out of the house if necessary.

'The door opened. Of its own accord,' she whispered, trying out the innocent–surprised pose she'd seen so often on the haunted house show. The cabinet shuddered, as if on cue, and a drawer fell open.

'Is this the spirit of Zebediah F Flanagan,' JJ Moon whispered to camera, 'turned poltergeist?'

Peta put a finger to her lips and handed JJ Moon the camera. It was time for the psychic to shine. 'Reveal yourself, spirit. Who are you – and do you mean us harm?'

They waited. At a silent nod, Dad and Rex moved the cabinet ... revealing Wulfie, mid chew, behind it.

'My beanie!' screamed Peta.

Wulfie dropped it instantly, reversing away and bumping the cabinet again. Another door popped open and out rolled a stash of hair dye. He had been trying to keep out of sight, as Libby had told him to, but all his stomachs had woken up again. Everyone was having breakfast so he'd thought that the bathroom would be an okay place to hide while he ate, but with all the chewing and the yummy taste of wet wool, he'd forgotten to stay small. Bit by bit, he had grown back to his normal medium-puppy size and this was why the cabinet had moved.

'Sorry,' said Libby, scooping Wulfie up. 'He didn't mean any harm.'

Peta, who wasn't very fond of dogs, snatched her hat and took the camera back from JJ Moon, who was frowning most peculiarly at Wulfie. 'You look just like the dog that strange woman said could talk ...'

Wulfie, sensibly enough, did not reply. That 'strange woman' had been Veronika's sister, Ilda, who was now in prison.

'How strange. Oh well, no harm done,' said the presenter and, 'Peta, a word. Upstairs.'

Veronika's fingers curled around Libby's upper arm, holding her there until JJ Moon, Peta and Dad had safely left the room. 'I won't be made a fool of on national TV,' she hissed at her step-daughter.

'Like Aunt Ilda,' said Rex. This was a mistake.

'I am *not* my sister,' said Veronika, showing him her fine white teeth. Rex decided to go for a very large breakfast immediately. 'When we move house—'

Libby gasped. 'You said you wouldn't sell!'

Veronika laughed. 'Of course I'm selling this horrible house. But here's the deal. If this house is haunted and features on this show, we bring the dog with us. If not ...' Veronika leant down, staring into Libby's eyes. 'We won't even leave him behind,' she said. 'I'll just send him to the pound or drop him down a well. Is that perfectly clear, even to a runt like you?'

'Perfectly,' said Libby, trying to keep her voice from shaking.

—

JJ Moon closed the door of the spare room behind him and leant against it. 'That dog, why haven't we seen it around the house before now?'

Peta frowned, not sure of the right answer. 'Because they've kept him hidden?' She might have been psychic but she wasn't sure where this line of questioning was going.

'So they could *use* him,' said the presenter. 'Who in this house could run as fast as that cold orb you saw last night?

'The dog?'

'Exactly. The father's an inventor and a damned good one – he could easily have rigged something up and tied it to the dog's back. As for that smell ... and the sounds ... and the drop in temperature ...'

'But I heard vibrations. There's something here, I'm sure of it!'

'Is there, Peta?' said JJ Moon, striking the questioning pose he'd perfected. 'Or have we been duped?'

—

Libby walked upstairs, past the closed door of the spare room, and sat on her bed. Wulfie wrapped his tail around her, looking as sorry as could be. 'I'll stay here,' he said. 'Quiet as anything.'

Libby shook her head slowly. 'I'm not losing you again, Wulfie.' She picked up the old hat, removing the second-last broken peacock feather. 'It's time to give Veronika a real haunted house.'

Chapter 19

'What about the rest of the interviews?' Veronika was as angry as an enormous storm that had been stuffed into a small jar. Her face had changed to a vivid pink colour and her hands were clenching and unclenching. This made the ghosts painted on her nails appear in a 'now you see it, now you don't' sort of way that was making Peta nervous. 'And the night shoot out in the back garden – it's a full moon tonight!'

'Not my call,' said Peta, avoiding eye contact and focusing on winding up all the extension leads. The laptop and most of the cameras had already been disconnected and put away.

Veronika stomped out of the room and caught JJ Moon leaving the bathroom. A bit like her son, Rex,

Libby's stepmother had a simple means of getting someone's undivided attention – she blocked the stairs so they couldn't pass.

'We cover *genuine* hauntings,' said JJ Moon, trying to avoid a scene.

'Are you suggesting—?' Veronika's eyes blazed. She took a deep breath. 'What about the rabbit in Rex's bed this morning?'

'You could have left it there.'

'The voices he heard,' said Veronika. 'That *I* heard. The bump in the wall. The ring of dampness!'

'The nail pierced one of your water pipes. You probably need to get a plumber out.'

'No. Your assistant ...' said Veronika. 'Last night—'

'Inconclusive,' said the presenter. 'Your husband's an inventor. Could have been a dry-ice device attached to the dog.'

'That thing?' said Veronika. 'I'd sooner haunt myself!'

JJ Moon needed to get back upstairs to pack his bag. He laid a hand on her arm to move her sideways. 'Look, we should have done more research. Your house might be haunted, but I'm sorry, I'm not convinced and we can't waste any more time on it.'

'But there *is* a ghost,' said Libby from the bottom of the stairs. She took a deep breath. This was possibly the most important speech of her life. 'He just doesn't like people looking for him because he's shy.'

'Is this true?' JJ Moon turned to Veronika.

Libby nodded imperceptibly and Veronika choked out a quiet, 'Yes'.

'If you stay for tea, but pretend you're not ghost hunters or anything,' said Libby, 'you might see him. I've laid everything out in the sitting room.'

'It might be worth it,' said Peta from the spare-room doorway. 'One last try. Since we're here.'

'I'll keep Wulfie with me the whole time, so you'll know it's not him,' said Libby. 'And *Mum*'s made a very special cake.'

JJ Moon was partial to cake and *not* partial to scenes. 'OK,' he said gruffly. 'But we need to keep filming.'

'Then pretend you're filming us all having tea,' said Libby. 'Point your camera at the cake?'

When they had all gone ahead into the sitting room, Libby hunched down in front of Wulfie. 'Ready?' she said.

Wulfie grinned. 'Very!'

—

Veronika refused to cut the cake until it was captured on camera, but then, while it was being doled out, Peta adjusted the tripod to get a view of the rest of the room. Libby had drawn the curtains to add to the atmosphere.

'There's generally a smell before he appears,' she said, helping herself to two large slices of chocolate cake and giving one to Wulfie.

Veronika could do nothing except smile and keep passing round the plates.

Nobody felt much like speaking, but they were sort of looking around and waiting while Wulfie ate as quickly as he could. Sweet things made him smell bad and, therefore, within moments, the room was filled with a smell so utterly awful that hands involuntarily pinched noses shut.

Veronika looked smug and sickened at the same time. 'Oh yes,' she said. 'There it is.'

Then, while everyone was looking left and right and somewhere else, Libby tickled Wulfie's nose with the peacock feather. He sneezed – and everyone froze.

Time had stopped.

'Right,' said Libby. 'Let's get ghosting!'

Quick as she could, Libby turned Veronika's picture upside down, while Wulfie lodged one of Rex's fingers in Rex's right ear and another up Rex's nose.

Peta's eye blinked.

'Quick,' said Libby. 'It's wearing off.'

Wulfie leapt into Libby's arms for another nose tickle and sneezed again.

This time, he put JJ Moon's coaster on top of his cup of tea and turned the whole lot upside down, while Libby moved the urn to Veronika's lap. Then Wulfie put Peta's shoes on the wrong feet, gave Veronika's nose an enormously wet lick topped with a smudge of chocolate icing, before moving on to Rex.

Her purple friend was moving around the room so fast, Libby could hardly see him and entirely missed him picking up the red marker pen Peta used to write up her notes. But she snatched Wulfie back just in time when she saw Veronika's nose twitch. By then he had finished the cake on everyone's plates and dropped an extra-large slice onto Dad's.

As time resumed, Libby was biting into her slice of cake with Wulfie sitting at her feet, trying not to smile.

Veronika put the urn down as if it was made of ants and her finger went to her nose. It was sticky. When the red marker slipped out from behind Wulfie's ear, Libby gently kicked it over towards Peta's chair, where the investigator might think she had dropped it.

'How extraordinary.' JJ Moon moved towards Veronika. Her hair had been woven into the shape of a tall ship, all masts and rigging, just like the painting of the young woman by the bathroom. Libby recognised what looked like the silk ribbon from the trunk in the hairdo, and could those be some of Dad's biscuits in the prow and stern?

She looked at Wulfie, who shook his head, as surprised as she was.

'A nineteenth-century schooner,' said JJ Moon. 'Outstanding work.'

Veronika stood up to look in the mirror and froze.

'Is this confirmation that the ghost is Zebediah?' pondered JJ Moon to the camera. He lifted his cup for a sip, drenching the front of his trousers with hot tea.

Rex stopped laughing when both investigators turned to him and stared. As did his mother, her face paler than a tub of melted vanilla ice-cream. 'Why are you all staring at me?' he asked.

Libby hid a snigger inside a pretend cough. Across Rex's forehead was written the word *Dimbo*.

'A mischievous spirit,' said Peta, handing JJ Moon a cloth. 'Would that fit with what you know about Zebediah?'

'Oh, said Veronika, through gritted teeth, 'yes. Yes, he certainly was.' She started scrubbing at Rex's forehead with a wet wipe.

'I guess that's what happens,' said Libby, trying not to grin, 'when you disturb a ghost.'

The wipe was working well. Rex's forehead now merely said *Dim*.

But then everything changed. Veronika pointed at Libby. 'YOU did this!'

Libby picked Wulfie up and shook her head. Too late, she realised she should have made sure to be near the door.

Veronika spun round to Dad, who was putting the urn back on the mantelpiece. 'Did you see what she did?'

'Oh. I don't think any of us saw her do anything,' said Dad.

This didn't stop Libby's stepmother. 'She's possessed!' shrieked Veronika. 'The ghost is inside her!'

Rex whimpered and Veronika turned back to the matter of his decorated forehead.

While Veronika was distracted, Libby made her way slowly around the table towards the door and Peta took JJ Moon aside. 'The girl did tell us what to do – and she made the ghost reveal himself ...'

'You think she's channelling the ghost – that it's speaking through her?' said JJ Moon.

Peta nodded. She'd heard of such things but never seen them in the flesh.

Libby was mere footsteps from the door when Peta stepped in front of her. 'Can you summon him again?' she asked. Libby shook her head. 'Ideally in physical form,' said Peta, 'so we can talk to him?'

Suddenly Libby didn't care what happened to the house. All she wanted to do was go upstairs with Wulfie and keep him safe. The lines around Peta's eyes weren't laughter lines. They were greed lines. The sort you get from always wanting more. If Libby could summon a ghost, she would have had him scare Peta and JJ Moon out of the house, light bulbs trailing down their backs like luminous tails.

'I didn't do anything—'

Veronika took JJ Moon's arm. 'Can't you exorcise her? Scare the spirit out of her or something?'

Libby took a deep breath. This wasn't going as she'd planned.

At all.

Chapter 20

Peta and JJ Moon were in a huddle by the door. Unable to leave, Libby kept back, watchful. Veronika was between her and Dad, so there really was nowhere to go. She buried her face in Wulfie's fur and whispered in his ear. 'First chance you get, run to our room and hide until they're all gone,' she said. 'If you have to, go out on the roof and hide there. Or go to Nazim's, he'll keep you safe.'

'We're so close,' Peta was saying. 'We merely need to make the poltergeist *polter* a bit.'

'Is that even a word?' said JJ Moon, adjusting his bow-tie and feeling uncomfortable.

'Not yet,' said Peta. 'But you know what I mean.'

'Not really,' interrupted Veronika, who hated to be left out of a private conversation.

'She means there's no use in a tame poltergeist,' said JJ Moon. 'A poltergeist that invisibly weaves your hair is not as exciting as one we can see on camera throwing things about.'

'I think your daughter is the key,' said his assistant to Veronika. 'If we can make her angry, Zebediah might appear through her, providing us with visual proof of paranormal possession – right here in Dublin!'

'Let me get this straight,' said Veronika. 'You want me to be mean to Libby?'

'Well,' said Peta, 'it wouldn't be as effective from one of us.'

'And then you'll exorcise her?'

'It might not be necessary,' said Peta. 'Sometimes ghosts, once they get to express themselves, are quite happy to leave their hosts.'

Veronika flexed her fingers like the arms of a small mechanical octopus and tried to look as if she was having to think about it. Right now, though, she was in exactly the right mood to be mean, and Libby, as far as she was concerned, had it coming. 'Jack, dearest,' she said to Libby's dad. 'Could you possibly go and put the kettle on? And make some sandwiches while you're down there? We might be here some time.'

'I'll do it,' said Libby, moving towards the door.

'Oh no, dear.' Veronika's hand clutched Libby's elbow and steered her away. 'Let your father do it.'

As soon as Dad had left, Peta led Libby to the centre of the room and positioned her directly in the camera's eyeline. 'Is it your mother who makes you angry?' she said.

'No,' said Libby quietly, holding Wulfie in her arms. 'My mother loves me.'

It was true, as far as she knew. Deep down in her heart, she knew her real mother would feel that way, wherever she had mislaid herself. Peta hadn't twigged that Veronika wasn't Libby's real mum, or that Veronika was meaner to Libby than anyone should be to anyone.

Peta turned to Veronika, her back to Libby. 'Ready to go?' she mouthed.

Veronika nodded. 'For the good of the show.'

Veronika turned towards her step-daughter. 'Oh, Libby Lou,' she said, petting Libby's hair.

Libby flinched. This had only happened once before, and then by accident. It was far scarier than Veronika being mean. Libby stepped back and put Wulfie down so her stepmother couldn't hurt him.

'Admit it,' said Veronika softly. 'You've always envied Rex. You wanted everything he had, including me!'

Libby almost laughed.

'Your brother the usurper,' said Peta, like a monkey on Veronika's shoulder. 'The boy who stole your mother's heart and home!'

'No!' said Libby. This was madness.

JJ Moon took Peta aside. 'Should we be doing this?'

'You want a show that will blow people's minds?' said Peta.

'She's only ten,' said the presenter.

'And this is TV.' Peta nodded to Veronika, who moved in on her step-daughter – the way she often had before, but never on a TV show with an audience of millions and with the full permission of its producers.

'Admit it,' said Veronika. 'You're feeling angry. Murderous. You want Rex to pay for your misdeeds. For your stupidity. Jealous, that's what you are. Jealous of your magnificent step-brother.'

Tired of saying no, Libby shook her head. Again and again. Her pigtails went to the left and the right, over and over.

'You can't face that Rex is a genius and you are nothing but a runt, a ... a ...' Veronika searched for the right word and found the one that would hurt most because it was her father's pet name for her. 'A MOUSE!'

'Stop it. Stop it. STOP IT!' Libby was crying. She couldn't help it. 'I'm just *me* and I don't hate anyone, not even you and not even Rex. All I want is for everyone not to be mean and horrible to me for no reason at all!'

'*That's* all you want?' Veronika's voice crackled. 'You lying, lazy waste of space! You—'

Wulfie snapped. 'Leave her alone!'

Somewhere a door slammed and the lights went out.

Libby went pale as Wulfie grew and grew until he towered over her tormentors.

In two quick chomps, Wulfie snapped up Veronika and Peta. Just like that.

On camera.

'No!' said Libby, staring.

Seeing the fear in his best friend's eyes, Wulfie shrank back down, as small as a chocolate pudding left overnight in the oven. As he shrank, his stomachs emptied out onto the carpet. Peta came out first. Second to be swallowed, she'd only reached the first of Wulfie's rumbling, tumbling tummies and was now covered in a thin bluish goop. A handful of Stinky Sigustingbugs were nestling in her left ear. Feeling daylight, they screamed instinctively.

To shut them up, Peta fell to the floor and rolled back and forth, squishing the slimy creatures into the carpet.

Veronika was less lucky. First to be swallowed, and being naturally slim and pointy, she had sped down Wulfie's throat into the second of his tummies without obstruction and now emerged a luminous shade of green.

'*Bluh, blurgh, glurgh* ...' Veronika spat out a number of Mooshyguts – long, thin and hairy, like one-armed slugs, they slid quickly away under the sofa – before plucking several Sigustingbugs from her tongue with her long nails. She did this with such vehemence that she stumbled backwards, bumping her head on the mantelpiece and folding down into the fireplace.

At this point, the urn tumbled off the mantelpiece, covering her entirely with the ashes she had instructed Libby to fill it with only the day before.

Rex missed it all.

The shock of seeing his mum swallowed had been too much. He was out cold, sucking his thumb, *im* still scribbled across his forehead.

JJ Moon punched the air. 'Now *that's* what I call ectoplasm!' He patted Libby on the head as he took in Veronika covered in green goo and ash, and Peta with her blue layer of slime.

'Thank you,' he said. 'You are wonderful. Sorry they were so mean.'

Chapter 21

Libby was halfway to her room by the time Peta had wiped enough slime off her face and hands to check what her camera had actually captured.

'I'm sorry,' said Wulfie, once Libby had shut the door behind them.

She answered him with a hug. The sort of hug a bear would give you if it was a comfort blanket rather than enormous and wild. Then she dragged her desk in front of the door and sat down on the bed to think. The lights going out wouldn't save them. Wulfie had already spoken by then, and Peta's camera had night vision. It would have caught Wulfie growing and swallowing and spitting and shrinking ...

Maybe Wulfie could hide at Nazim's house – but what would Nazim's parents think, and what if one of his neighbours saw Wulfie and told the papers? Maybe it would be safer to tell Wulfie to go off by himself – but would anywhere be safe once that footage was shown on TV? Everyone would be looking for him.

Libby made a promise to herself and to Wulfie. She would keep him hidden. They had done it before when he'd first tumbled out of Zebediah's trunk.

They could do it again.

—

Downstairs, Peta swore. Until the beast had materialised – for she was thinking of it as a beast now, not a ghost – the image was crystal clear. Then the screen clouded up, as if something had deliberately and electronically interfered with the video reception at the very moment that Wulfie spoke.

'There!' JJ Moon pointed at the corner of the screen behind Peta where a purple smudge had materialised, seconds before the screen dissolved into grey lines of interference. The audio was working again, however, so they heard the swallowing and munching and spewing.

Peta felt ill.

Only when both swallowees had been regurgitated back up Wulfie's throat onto the carpet and the lights had come on again did the image on the screen become clear, and then—

'What's that?' said JJ Moon.

Behind Veronika and Peta was a tall, bearded shadow in a large hat with feathers. Clear as anything – for a shadow, that is.

'Zebediah,' said Dad, breathing out slowly.

And then they heard audio from the recording that nobody had heard before: '*Leave my house alone.*'

'Congratulations,' said JJ Moon to an astonished Veronika. 'You have a real ghost and we have a winning show!'

—

Libby was packing her WonderWulf knapsack with the things Wulfie might need, like an umbrella and most of her socks, in case he had to hide on the roof. 'If you wear the socks for a while, they'll get a bit smelly,' she said, 'and then you can eat them.' She was adding the last few of Dad's biscuits from the tin when a knock on the door made her jump and drop the bag.

'Can I come in, Mouse?'

Libby moved the desk away from the door and let Dad in. He handed her the old rug – 'You might like this back' – and sat down on her bed. Stroking Wulfie between the ears, he told her all about the footage they'd just seen. 'Apart from Zebediah's appearance, nothing else can be seen clearly at all. They said it was as if something – maybe old Zebbie himself – interfered with the recording. Upshot is that the house will feature on their show after all. They're just filming a few links and bits and bobs and then they'll be gone.'

Wulfie climbed up onto his lap and Dad sneezed. 'Oh dear,' he said, then, 'Could have been worse. Could have stopped time.'

'What did you say?' said Libby. Her father had a habit of mumbling and he seemed particularly mumbly tonight.

'The producer told me what Veronika did and I'm very sorry for that,' said Dad. 'Can't think why she doesn't like you the best. You're a much nicer variety of child than the boy.' He stood up and hugged her. 'I'm afraid it might be because you're mine.'

'I like being yours,' said Libby, hugging him back.

—

Peta and JJ Moon decided to stay another night after all, to film the interviews and pick-ups they'd originally planned. While they hooked up all the equipment again, Veronika soaked in the bath. By the time she was back downstairs lying on the sofa, Libby's stepmother had convinced herself, with some difficulty, that the whole experience had just been a bit of fun.

As in, *Silly old Zebediah. You knew what we needed, didn't you? We're ever so grateful. Now you can go back to being non-existent again.*

Veronika told Libby to bring in the remains of the cake. It was time to celebrate her achievements. Then she pushed a brochure over Dad's *Inventors Being Inventorish* magazine. 'Here, Jack,' she said. 'Isn't this the perfect home for us?'

'Considerably further away from St Bartholomew's,' said Dad. 'Won't that be inconvenient?'

'It's across the road from Tuffington Academy for darling Rex,' huffed Veronika. 'So what if Libby has to walk a couple of miles to school? Exercise is important for children.'

'Isn't Rex a child too?' Dad said, smiling at Libby as she carried in what was left of the cake and a large pot of tea.

'Geniuses are different,' said Veronika. 'They need to protect their brains from excessive exercise and air.' She cut an especially large slice of cake for Rex, a sliver for Dad, an extra-large piece for herself and none at all for Libby. 'You can put the rest back in the fridge,' she said to Libby.

Dad lowered his magazine and sniffed. Loudly.

Veronika flinched and looked around her, every fibre alert for paranormal beasts.

'What's that smell?' he said.

Veronika sniffed timidly, as if expecting to be ecto-plasmed at any moment.

Dad sipped his tea. 'Not that it matters,' he said, 'since Zebediah only seems to appear when you're mean to Libby.'

Veronika held out her plate to Libby. Loudly, she said, in clipped syllables, 'Please have the largest slice of cake, Libby. It will help you grow up big and strong.'

Libby took it and said thank you very politely. She even added 'Mum' to make the experience a little less traumatic for her stepmother.

—

Veronika managed to smile at JJ Moon when he came to join them. He helped himself to a large cup of tea and pointed at a panel on the left-hand side of the fireplace. 'Was that always there?'

Dad moved over to take a look, stroking the ship carved into the wood. Libby had never seen it before – most likely because a section of the fireplace had folded away into the wall, leaving it revealed.

'When you bumped your head, my dear,' Dad said to Veronika, 'you must have hit a hidden lever. How clever of you!'

Veronika liked to feel clever – and what if the panel hid a secret stash of pirate gold? Pushing Dad aside, she slid her long nails along the edge of it until the panel clicked open. She pulled out a leather pouch that was disappointingly flat and full of paper so she handed it to Dad.

JJ Moon had called Peta down, so he was there with his camera when Dad laid the pouch on the table. He felt the initials ZFF engraved into the leather. 'I think it belonged to my great-grandfather,' he said.

'Not ... *Zebediah*?' whispered Veronika, looking nervous.

'Oh yes.' Dad unwound the leather ties. Inside was a map of no place they could identify and a set of documents. Libby stood at his side, recognising the writing from the recipe book, full of curls and swirls like waves on a sea. 'It's his Last Will & Testament,' said Dad. 'Story was that he had put it somewhere safe but nobody could ever find it.'

'May I?' said JJ Moon, who loved old documents.

'The house is ours now,' said Veronika, 'whatever the will says. It's out of date, right?'

'I'm not so sure,' said the presenter slowly. 'Zebediah says he's leaving the house and everything in it, in perpetuity – which means forever – to the first daughter of each generation, unless there are no daughters. In that case a son can own it, but as a guardian, holding it safe for the next generation. I've never seen anything like this.'

'That won't stop us selling the house,' said Veronika.

'Oh yes,' said Dad, grinning at Libby. 'I think it might. You see, technically, it would seem that I don't really own the house at all, so you can't either, despite being my wife. The real owner of the house would appear to be Libby, so selling or not, it's up to her.'

'And I really don't want to sell this house,' said Libby. 'It's my home, and I love everything about it!'

—

Libby was floating on air by the time she returned to her room. She didn't even notice that the first roll of fresh cream wallpaper had begun to detach itself from the wall outside her room. It would take weeks but slowly, surely, the house would eventually go back to the way Libby liked it, although she didn't know that yet.

The official excuse would be damp. (Though she and Wulfie were pretty sure it was because Zebediah didn't like the cream-coloured wallpaper either.)

Libby wasn't sure how her owning the house would change things – although she was certain it would – so the sensible thing to do seemed to be to carry on as normal, at least until Veronika calmed down. It had been a very long few days but before she went to bed, since Zebediah had trusted her with all this, Libby had one more very important task: to clean Rex's doodles off the ship picture she loved.

She sat down beside Wulfie on the bed and carefully, using the side of her scissors, eased the painting from its frame. A small photo fell out of the back of the picture frame and landed at her feet. It was a formal portrait taken in a studio, with a backdrop of a palm tree and the sea. The subject was a very tall man in the hat that was currently sitting on Libby's bed, now empty of feathers, and he was wearing a cape that looked very similar to the red velvet one in the trunk.

He also had a long beard that split into two waves and reached down to the turned-up toes of a pair of black leather boots. In his hand was the watch-that-wasn't. 'Look, Wulfie,' said Libby. 'It must be Zebediah!'

Wulfie climbed onto her lap and they both stared at the photo. 'I feel as if we already met,' said Wulfie, stifling a little yawn.

'Me too,' said Libby, yawning herself. Yawns can be contagious that way.

'Do you think he made Veronika's hair into a ship?'

Libby grinned. 'I'm guessing so.'

Noticing that the photo was stuck to something else, Libby prised it apart. It was a second studio photo with the same setting, but in this painting Zebediah was nose to nose with something that looked rather like a wulfen ...

Libby grinned and hugged Wulfie tight. 'I think he knew about the trunk.'

'I'm not the only wulfen who came here!' said Wulfie, feeling better for knowing this.

'Maybe everyone who owns this house has a wulfen friend?' said Libby. She turned the picture over and showed it to Wulfie so he could see the name of the wulfen with Zebediah.

'Wolfgang Amadeus Rachmaninoff!' he read. 'That's who I'm named after! He disappeared before my great-grandfather was born.'

They sat there looking at the photo for the longest time, thinking about what all this meant. That Zebediah had known about the portal; that he'd appeared today to protect them and to make sure that his great-great-grand-daughter didn't lose her best friend *or* her home.

'You and me,' said Libby, putting the photo and the painting onto her desk for now, 'we were meant to find each other and take care of each other.' She curled up on the bed with Wulfie in her arms. 'I can't wait to tell Nazim,' she managed, before the two best friends fell soundly – and very contentedly – asleep.

Acknowledgements

Finally, a ghost story – of sorts! I have always been interested in ghosts, having seen my first one aged seven, though the nuns weren't too happy when I tried to hold a séance on the back steps of my primary school aged ten! When I wasn't trying to summon spirits, I invented a language with its own alphabet and spied through the hedge to see if any of our neighbours were witches. But other than that, my head was buried in books: torches under the bedclothes, head in another world.

Just as it has been during this pandemic, in the world of Libby and Wulfie.

I wrote this book mostly marooned in one room after two leg operations, one of which meant I couldn't walk for sixteen weeks. My imagination went into overdrive, spinning so many possible twists and turns and bits of daftness. So thank you to Dee Barragry, Stephanie Lee, Nicola Lindsay and Libby Sedgwick for letting me talk through the questions I had.

Thanks also to Hayley Stevens for her invaluable advice on paranormal investigators and to Catherine Kuhlmann for advice on the plumbing in an old house.

On behalf of all the Wulfie books, I'd like to thank all the reviewers, bloggers and retweeters across social media, and the bookshops and libraries that have stocked my books. As for the readers, no book exists without you. I'd especially like to thank Jazzy Henry and Finn Simpson, two readers whose love of Wulfie encouraged me, and also Laura Lee Mooney, Antoinette Fennell, Ellie Lundy and all the other mums and teachers who have read Wulfie to and with their children.

Finally, a huge thank you to Rosa Devine for her fantastic and imaginative illustrations and to all at Little Island Books – Elizabeth Goldrick, Kate McNamara, Matthew Parkinson Bennett and Siobhán Parkinson – and to my editor, Venetia Gosling, an enormous hug and a thank you for loving Wulfie as much as I do.

We hope you have enjoyed reading *Wulfie: A Ghostly Tail*, the fourth book in the *Wulfie* series by Lindsay J Sedgwick.

The following pages will introduce you to the other books in the *Wulfie* series, which you might also like to read.

www.littleisland.ie

WULFIE: STAGE FRIGHT
By Lindsay J Sedgwick
Illustrated by Josephine Wolff

Libby longs to star in the school play. When she finds a little purple creature called Wulfie in an old chest in her bedroom, Libby discovers a new best friend who just might help her outshine her big bad brother, Rex.

Wulfie: Stage Fright is available to buy from all good bookshops and online from the Little Island website **littleisland.ie/books/wulfie-stage-fright/**

Learn more about your favourite characters and their adventures at the Wulfie series website **littleisland.ie/wulfie/**

WULFIE: BEAST IN SHOW

By Lindsay J Sedgwick

Illustrated by Josephine Wolff

Aunt Ilda is coming to visit, and that means big trouble for Libby and her adorable purple best friend, Wulfie. Ilda will do anything to win the top dog show prize on live TV. Anything. Including kidnapping Wulfie!

But Wulfie, of course, isn't a dog at all. He talks, he shrinks and grows, and when he sneezes – time freezes. He's the sweetest best friend Libby could hope for – and now he needs her help.

Can Libby rescue Wulfie and humiliate Aunt Ilda on TV? Well, with a best friend like Wulfie, anything can happen.

Wulfie: Beast in Show is available to buy from all good bookshops and online from the Little Island website **littleisland.ie/books/wulfie-beast-show**

WULFIE
SAVES THE PLANET
By Lindsay J Sedgwick

Illustrated by Rosa Devine

Libby only has three days to create the best ever eco-project for school. So the last thing she needs is Wulfie showing off his 'super' powers, like changing size and stopping time with his sneezes.

Nasty Rex is plotting to get rid of Wulfie and the pressure is piling up on Libby. But Wulfie has a super plan to save the planet – and he might just save himself and Libby's project too.

After all, with a best friend like Wulfie, anything can happen!

Wulfie Saves The Planet is available to buy from all good bookshops and online from the Little Island website **littleisland.ie/books/wulfie-saves-planet**

Free Fun Wulfie Games and Activities

At Little Island we love the Wulfie series as much as you do! We've created a collection of Wulfie activities so you can draw, write, play and even act out your favourite moments from the series.

They are all free and available to download at **littleisland.ie/wulfie/**

 Make your own dress-up masks of best
friends Libby and Wulfie

Download cut-out masks of the best friends to play with!

Act out a scene from Wulfie's life with a short play script

Find the Wulfie-related words in our wordsearch

Colour a picture of Wulfie and Libby singing to the night sky

Lots of other fun games and activities await on **littleisland.ie**, including writing guides to help you create your own scenes from Wulfie's world!

ABOUT LINDSAY J SEDGWICK

Lindsay is an award-winning screenwriter and creator of *Punky*, the first mainstream animation series worldwide in which the central character has special needs (Down's syndrome). A former journalist, she has written for film and TV, games and apps, and the stage. She is currently adapting her first novel for TV, brainstorming mad ideas she hopes will be books and being distracted by her new muse, a white and black cat called Beanz.

www.lindsayjsedgwick.com

ABOUT ROSA DEVINE

Rosa is an illustrator, educator and designer who likes to draw things, make things and bake things. In the winter she has the honour of teaching bright, sparkling young minds and in the summer she makes comics and oil paintings. Rosa lives in Dublin, surrounded by tottering piles of books and free-range paintbrushes.

www.rosadevine.com

ABOUT LITTLE ISLAND

Founded in 2010 in Dublin, Ireland, Little Island Books publishes good books for young minds, from toddlers all the way up to older teens. In 2019 Little Island won a Small Press of the Year award at the British Book Awards. As well as publishing a lot of new Irish writers and illustrators, Little Island publishes books in translation from around the world.

Little
Island
Books create waves

RECENT AWARDS WON BY LITTLE ISLAND BOOKS

Savage Her Reply by Deirdre Sullivan

Winner: An Post Irish Book Awards Dept 51 @ Eason Teen
and Young Adult Book of the Year 2020

Winner: KPMG Children's Books Ireland Awards
Book of the Year Award 2021

Winner: Biennial Literacy Association of Ireland
Young Adult Book Award 2021

The Gone Book by Helena Close

Winner: White Raven Award 2021

The Deepest Breath by Meg Grehan

Winner: KPMG Children's Books Ireland Awards
Judge's Special Award 2020

Shortlisted: Waterstones Children's Book Prize 2020

Dangerous Games by James Butler

Winner: Great Reads Awards 2020

Mucking About by John Chambers

Selected for the IBBY Honours List 2020